Strange Sands Suspense 1
Hilton Head

The Old Cedar Chest

Pamela Poole
Southern Sky Publishing

eBook ISBN: 9781956089141
ISBN: 9781956089158
Print ISBN: 9781956089165

Author's Note

Have you ever walked into a place and instantly became ill at ease? Did you ever meet a person and your spirit clashed with his or hers? Was there ever a time when you couldn't explain it, but you simply knew something bad might happen at any moment—and it did?

The novellas in the Strange Sands Suspense series will follow the adventures of a young lady named Mercedes Ellison, whose family has a long history of unexplainable encounters that many would call "strange." But then, Christians are peculiar people who should be living supernatural lives.

The stories and people in this series are fictional, but they are steeped in places I've been, situations I've experienced, and people I interviewed who have had these encounters—encounters they typically keep to themselves. Each story will contain at least one of the events from my interviews. I hope you'll enjoy the Southern Lowcountry ambiance in this series, where moments spent on warm sandy beaches blend with the grains of slipping sand in history's hourglass.

Prologue

I'm not afraid of the devil. The devil can handle me - he's got judo
I never heard of. But he can't handle the One to whom I'm
joined;
he can't handle the One to whom I'm united;
he can't handle the One whose nature dwells in my nature.
-A.W. Tozer

In England, in the Year of Our Lord 1900

Claire Ellison felt the familiar rush of adrenaline that alerted her to a battle being waged. She looked up from the Bible in her lap to the dying flames in the hearth. "What?" she whispered.

She waited for some sort of revelation, direction, or conviction, and sat motionless, silencing the comforting creak of her old rocking chair. Her heart suddenly jumped with anticipation and flooded with confidence. Her hands trembled, not with fear, but with boldness and courage.

The house maid came to the door. "Do you need anything before we tuck the house in for the evening?" She saw Claire's eyes and kneeled beside the arm of the chair. "Miss Claire, how can I help?"

"You can alert the staff to be watchful. I'm not sure why, but I hope they will humor an old woman." She smiled and closed the leather volume, handing it to the maid. Then she rose slowly from the rocking chair. "Please go get Varon and be ready for the emergency plan."

The maid gasped, her eyes like saucers as she rushed to place the old family Bible on the honey-colored wooden top of the side table. But Claire said, "Take it with you, dear. It must leave here with Mercedes."

Flustered, the maid hugged the leather book close and rushed to say, "Of course, Miss Claire."

A clamor of horse's hooves and shouts came from the front courtyard, and then a frantic pounding on the thick doors. The maid moved protectively toward her mistress as the butler appeared to open them. Breathless, they listened as two of the night watch guards reported that a group of riders was on the way. "They ride with an evil purpose," blurted the eldest guard. "I sent young Tom to race his horse to town for help by the short path. He won't be back in time!"

Claire gave the house maid a nod that sent her running down the hall, choking on a sob as she cried out for Claire's granddaughter. Then Claire moved as if she were many years younger, stepping closer to the door to speak to the guard. "You did the best thing. Raise the alarm all over the estate."

The guard nodded to his companion, who turned to leap from the porch, then he stood with his bulk filling the doorway and sputtered. His eyes pleaded. "You must leave, Miss Claire! Varon is getting the tunnel ready for you and your granddaughter."

He read her eyes before her lips spoke, and he groaned in dread before he heard her soft voice. "I cannot. It's time the evil one is confronted and stopped, for he will never leave Mercedes in peace."

"May the Lord fight with us," the guard said gruffly, then spun on his heel to hasten to defenses. It did not seem odd to him that a sudden, rainless thunderstorm rumbled in the distance.

Seventeen-year-old Mercedes Ellison had spent the evening by the fire with her beloved grandmother before retiring to her room to write in her journal and read. But after putting down her pen and picking up a book, she became distracted and restless. The feeling of foreboding made her decide to check around the house for anything unusual before changing into her nightgown.

She nearly jumped at the housemaid's alarmed call for her. In a flash, she pulled on her shoes, and the door to her bedroom burst open. The flushed maid's eyes were wild as she rushed into the room, clutching the old family Bible. "Miss Mercedes, get your travel case and wrap! We must flee to the escape tunnel! Hurry!"

It was a memorized plan. Her family and the staff rehearsed it and kept prepared for using it, but this time, the maid's stifled terror told Mercedes this was no drill. "Has my grandmother already gone to meet Varon?" she asked, snatching up the journal on her desk while the maid gathered her bag and cloak.

"She revealed no plans, Miss, only told me to get you there right away, and I won't fail her. I won't fail her!" she declared as she pushed Mercedes out the door. "Quick, there's no time to lose!"

Horses reigned in, their riders gathering behind their leader. The torches carried by five of the riders created eerie shadows that looked like frenzied demons dancing in the courtyard of the Ellison estate. The leader's saddle creaked as he shifted to lean forward, giving a boost from his body to amplify his shout. "Ellison, come out!"

A handful of armed men silently appeared from the shadows around the large house and stables, their rifles poised and ready. Soft lights glowed in the windows downstairs, spilling through the double front doors as they were opened. Claire Ellison nodded to her butler to move away from the doors, and she stood there alone, straight, tall, looking years younger and stronger when framed by the romance of lamplight in the foyer.

The leader snarled, "Your son is traveling again, Mrs. Ellison? Carrying on the family name, doing good and fighting the everlasting war against evil?"

He was the only man who laughed, and it was a bitter sound. The figure in the doorway gracefully glided forward onto the porch in the whispers of her long skirt. Thunder made the ground tremble as she took the steps down to the courtyard and stood at the last one, bathed in a pool of moonlight that broke through the stirring clouds. Lightning flashed, revealing every dark corner, electrifying the nerves of the gathered men and horses.

When the lady of the house remained silent, some horses nickered, and men shifted in their saddles. Their leader finally growled, "You know why I'm here. Give me back my land."

A gust of wind stirred the trees and made the torch flames flicker violently. Men jerked their arms up to hold on to their hats as Claire's calm voice rang out. "You despised this land when you sold it to someone else, Mr. Lenoir, intending to swindle him. Everyone gathered here is a witness that it went through two owners before my husband received it in payment of a debt. You badgered them all after finding out it was not the wasteland you thought you were cheating them with. You've failed in every legal means to take it from us. When we are ready to sell it, you can make an offer, like any buyer."

"This land has been in my family for years!" boomed Lenoir. His horse balked and he struggled to get it under control. Then he leered at Claire. "If you won't give it back, I will take it, through my son and your granddaughter, in a scandal that results in unholy matrimony."

Several of the men in the shadows moved, but they stopped when Claire raised her hand. She stepped forward, and several electrified, lightning-bathed moments revealed the identities of the true adversaries. Gasps filled the courtyard.

Lenoir dismounted and took menacing strides to face Claire, whose chin rose in confidence. He demanded that she sign over the deed to his land. She said the document was not there to sign or to give him.

Enraged now, his roar mingled with crashing thunder. Horses whinnied, but they could not distract their riders from the scene before them. No one questioned if she told the truth, for this woman was not capable of anything less. Lenoir had a pistol pointed at her before the guards stationed in the shadows realized it, but then the shuffle and clicks of their aimed rifles filled the air. Her hand gestured to stay them, but they did not lower their weapons this time. She stood serene as she reminded Lenoir that she had no fear of him, for when she gave her heart to Jesus as a child, she had become a citizen of heaven. She declared it was not too late for him to do the same.

His expression dripped scorn and hatred. He snarled, "Tonight, I'm sending you to the eternal home you cherish so much!"

When the pistol shot rang out, lightning was splitting the heavens. Bright explosions and jarring shadows filled the courtyard. Horses reared, almost throwing their riders, and confusion reigned.

Swiftly, Claire reached into her waistband and drew out a silver dagger. A dark stain spread over the white lace on her dress as she plunged the blade into Lenoir's heart, crying out, "And I'm sending you to yours!"

Lenoir staggered back in stunned shock, then went to his knees. Claire swayed, remaining on her feet in triumph until he fell on his face. Then she crumpled to the flagstones while the butler ran down the steps to her aid. The last thing she did was to pull her silver dagger from Lenoir's heart.

A swirling wisp like a vapor rose from Lenoir's fallen form and hovered above the horsemen. Lenoir's horse reared, eyes rolling wildly, and raced from the courtyard. The other riders dropped their torches. They fled on their spooked horses with the disembodied demon in pursuit.

Chapter 1

Life is a storm. You will bask in the sunlight one moment and be shattered on the rocks the next. What makes you a man is what you do when the storm comes.
-Edmond Dantes, The Count of Monte Cristo

Mercedes Annalee Ellison held her Great-Great Grand Aunt's fragile journal and a tattered manila envelope, puzzling about whether these items would change her life. Her intuition screamed that they would, and the way they had come into her possession would make any skeptic pause.

She wanted to bolt, to flee what loomed ahead.

Instead, she stood in her bedroom and looked up to meet her mother's eyes. "Sawyer found these in that old cedar chest?"

"They were behind a secret panel made to fit the lid," her mother replied. "He had to take it apart to restore the hinges."

"Dad, I wish you would open them."

Her dad's eyes sparkled. "Mercedes, these are yours to discover. You didn't know about that estate auction when you stopped; the auction personnel had no record of the cedar chest in their inventory; and a neighbor claims an unknown man unloaded it before the auction began. You felt drawn to it, never noticing the tarnished name plate."

"Grandpa Ellison claims the family lost track of this chest in the chaos of the air raids after Aunt Mercedes died," her mother added. "You've never heard of it, never saw photos of it. What do you believe about how this came into your possession?"

Mercedes hesitated. Unusual, even bizarre, occurrences were a watermark stamped on the Ellison family. This one had interrupted her packing for a few months' stay in a vacation cottage in Bluffton, South Carolina. Distractions were not welcome in her life right now. She had three great jobs lined up over the summer—and a problem with her boyfriend.

"Okay, I'll open the envelope first. Stay here with me," she said, putting the journal on the bed beside her yawning suitcase. Mercedes often handled old documents and expected the dry crackling sound as the seal relented to allow her invasion. Gently, she slid some aged yellowed documents out and studied the first two before looking up to meet the expectant eyes of her parents.

"This is a property deed," she announced. "I know this isn't your area of expertise, Dad. You should have an attorney familiar with British law look it over. Grandpa might know who the parties listed in the transaction were. There doesn't seem to have been any money exchanged because the land was payment of a debt."

Her father looked stunned as he took the papers from her and examined them. Almost to himself, he muttered, "After all these years..."

"Is this the land outside of London?" her mother asked, raising on her tiptoes to look over his shoulder.

"The survey seems to show that, but this looks unfamiliar, probably completed by a village government official. The date is what I'm guessing from, and my family name. They found some valuable minerals and gold on the land after this transaction, and then a man named Roland Lenoir wanted it back. He murdered Claire Ellison over it, but she had the strength to stab him with a mortal wound, sinking her silver dagger into his heart. She knew he was coming and sent her granddaughter Mercedes away with some friends and staff members. The deed was with her."

Mercedes solemnly picked up the journal and leafed through it while her parents looked over the sketchy legal documents. In her career as an architectural historian, she dealt with things like property transactions, wills, and other historical information. The people who had lived, died, and left a record of themselves were real. Her parents named her after the woman who left this part of her life behind.

"When I'm finished packing, I'll look this over and tell you about it."

Mercedes was ready for an early morning start, loaded with all she needed until she came back home to Charleston to visit. She walked back inside the house with her parents, ready to enjoy dinner with them, her grandparents, and her mother's sister and husband. Her brother Zeke could not get away from his hospital residency job, so he had called and made her laugh with the hilarious misadventures of doing a shift in the emergency room.

During dinner, her Grandpa Ellison talked about the journal. "When you read it, I'm interested in hearing your ancestor's account of what exactly happened to Claire Ellison," he said. "The report from witnesses at the scene, and the evidence found by the law enforcement that came out of town that night, paints an intriguing encounter of a clash between good and evil. A photocopy is in the family vault, if you ever want to read it."

Mercedes hesitated, and her father said, "Dad, I'm arranging an appointment with an attorney about the deeds and other papers in the envelope from the cedar hope chest. This is only a formality that will easily free up the land to donate or sell it. The trails and equestrian park are ready."

"It all sounds like a novel!" exclaimed Mercedes' aunt, and everyone laughed. Looking at her sister, she said, "Josette, I would have had my nose in that journal on the ride home from the shop. And Mercedes, when will that carpenter friend of yours finish work on the chest? Perhaps he'll find another treasure in it. What's his name again? Somethin' about a novel by Mark Twain."

Mercedes grinned and set down her water glass. "His name is Sawyer. We went to school together. He's a master at restoration and upcycling things for me and my clients, and he comes across hidden things that get me entangled in more mysteries than I want in my life."

"Speaking of clients, what's on your schedule this summer?" her uncle asked.

"I'll do research and paperwork for a society in Bluffton. I'm renting a place from a family acquaintance, in the historic downtown district. It isn't far from Savannah, where I'll work with a couple on a historic property they purchased. They plan to restore it and open it as an inn. In July, I'll be helping a family assess a plantation estate in Charleston that they inherited."

Her uncle beamed at her, then looked at her father. "She's going to make it just fine as an independent business, Dawson. Such an interesting career, too."

She smiled at the compliment and took a dainty bite from her plate. Her uncle had no idea she chose her career because it sounded safe and boring.

Mercedes slid wearily into bed. As she reached to turn off the lamp, her hand bumped into the cover of the old journal, a reminder that she told her parents she would look at it.

She sighed and left the lamp on, staring at the book, reluctant to open this bit of family history. Once she saw what was within the once-pretty, now-faded binding, she couldn't forget it. What she learned there would become part of her identity.

Prayer was a continual part of her life, not just a bedtime routine, and opening this journal was a weighty matter she held out before the Lord several times as she packed. She did so again now. Then she opened the little book.

Centered on the first page was her Great-Great Grand Aunt's name. On the next line were the words, *The Year of Our Lord Nineteen Hundred*. The ink had aged into a periwinkle tone on the creamy, expensive paper.

Quaint, thought Mercedes. She turned the page, and the beguiling scent of roses tickled her nose, then wafted away. She almost gasped at the sudden realization that the script looked as if she herself had written it.

The page seemed to be a memory tool for a family tree, though it wasn't a long one, due to space. Her aunt had written the names of her grandparents and parents, then her brother and herself. At the bottom, she wrote prettily, *Mercedes means mercies in Spanish, and my mother has Spanish heritage. She passed into heaven when I was fifteen. I am seventeen this year.*

Mercedes scanned the lines linking the family tree and sat up straight against the headboard of her bed. This young lady's grandmother was Claire Ellison, a woman who was handy with a silver dagger.

She turned the next several pages. If she discovered an account of Claire's murder, she would not read it. She wasn't ready. But the pages were brief lists of everyday things, like quotes her young aunt liked, books read, and scripture verses she was studying or memorizing. Then, there was a page that looked like a story, with the title *Silver and Garlic* centered on the header.

Mercedes yawned from weariness and knew she should sleep, but she was intrigued and settled into the comfort and fresh softness of her sheets and pillow. Her mind could only imagine one theme for a story about silver and garlic, and it was a dark one. As she scanned the first few lines of this one, however, she knew it was not fiction. Her aunt was recording a meaningful evening spent at home.

Earlier tonight, the rhythmic creaking in the joints of my grandmother's oak rocking chair sang like a lullaby as I sat cross-legged on a rug beside her. Her fingers weren't as nimble as they once were, but they were tenacious as she wove heavy twine around the tails of pairs of garlic bulbs that mimicked her knuckles. If a messenger came for a hushed visit with my father, he looped the braided twine through his belt and packed an extra one inside a case he always carried on mysterious journeys. Often, I went with him as far as the harbor to see him off. Someday, the case with the intriguing silver clasp of crossed swords will belong to my brother and I, and the thought sent a shiver down my spine.

My brother is far away at the university, studying medicine and law, like our father did. My father is on one of his journeys tonight, and soon, I'll be old enough to travel with him. But here, tonight, the cozy glow from the hearth embraced me and my beloved grandmother, sheltering us from a world that isn't safe.

For as long as I can remember, evenings like this one have been among the times when she prepared me for my unusual family legacy. I am a teenager now, and I stretched to settle more comfortably, anticipating one of her stories. But she seemed content with her own thoughts tonight, glancing up from her work to gaze into the merry flames as if she were somewhere else. She deftly handled an ancient, ornate silver dagger she kept sharp, cutting the ends of the corded twine. With a delicious shiver, I wondered about the ominous uses she may once have put that silver dagger to. When she lowered it into a basket and began another nest for two more garlic bulbs, I handed them up to her and ventured, "Grandma, tell me again about the legend of the garlic braids."

A transforming smile smoothed away her wrinkles, giving me a glimpse of the woman who has lived many adventures in places I've never been. Her tone was indulgent as she said, "Garlic is a gift from God, a remedy to help us heal. We should know how to use it as a medicine for ourselves and to help others. One bulb would be enough, but our family always binds up two together, because Jesus sent out the disciples two by two when He empowered them. He gave them authority over evil spirits. Where can you find that passage in the Bible?"

My eyes went to a thick volume of timeworn, cracking black leather, the family's copy of the Holy Scriptures. It was also a record of our generations, from our family surname, meaning My God is Yahweh. But a recital of the carefully hand-written names and dates on aging parchment was not what she asked for tonight. My tone sounded reverent in my own ears when I answered, "It's in the Gospels, in Mark, chapter six, verse seven."

My grandmother nodded. "Can you see the advantages of having a Christian companion in the world?"

I was the one who gazed into the fire now, gathering my recollected answers to this question from previous evenings. When I turned to look back, she was ready for two more bulbs with the long stems. I took them from the basket and held them up to her in my palm.

"Yes, ma'am," I responded, watching her nestle the pair in the heavy twine. "Ecclesiastes 4:9-12 describes it, as well. A friend holds you accountable for living as you should, giving you counsel about decisions, protecting you in the face of your enemies, taking on half of the work, encouraging you and strengthening your faith. Your friend is the witness to the times the Lord led you to overcome challenges, tragedy, and evil."

She smiled in satisfaction, her silvery gray hair gleaming in the firelight. I've always imagined that it radiates around her, like an aura, enhancing my vision of her as being otherworldly and living here as God's special agent on assignment in a place that doesn't deserve her. She raised a completed cord with one arm, studying the white garlic bulb duet that was encased there. In the firelight's glow, those homely garlic bulbs seemed to radiate with something of my grandmother's other worldliness, reminding me of the descriptions of how the righteous are clothed in spotless white linen.

"Those that Christ sends, He also equips," she said. "They abide in Him. Just as these are nestled in the strength of twine, a believer is secure in His protection. The braids are three strands, representing the Trinity—the Father, the Son, and the Holy Spirit. All three are who He is, yet they also work in their own way to envelop a child of God."

Setting the cord in the basket beside her rocking chair, my grandmother lifted her wrinkled hand to touch the silver cross that hung around her neck. Instinctively, I reached up for my own, and she waited for me to speak the words I learned before I could recall anything else.

"This cross is empty because Jesus Christ rose from the dead to conquer death forevermore," I said with reverence. "The silver metal fashioned into a cross shape on this necklace has no special power, but it stands as a symbol of Christ's victory and of the finished work of redemption, so His enemies despise it. The only true source of a Christian's power is Christ Himself, and in knowing the inspired scriptures that counter and dispel evil. Since Christ lives within us, as John 17:3 says, and heaven is His kingdom, we are citizens of heaven, here on earth."

Through the windows of our eyes, my grandmother's spirit and mine connected, and her expression was the one that always made my heart soar. It said she was pleased, and that she had confidence in me. "Grandma," I breathed, with another shiver of anticipation. You see, my favorite part was about to unfold. "Remind me again about why it's so vital that I remember all of this."

Now, her chin came up, giving me a glimpse of the resolve that had conquered evil in many forms during her long lifetime. A familiar flash lit the eyes that were the color of the green hills, meadows, brooks, and woods she had traveled years ago. When she spoke, her voice was clear and strong. "Scripture says our enemy is not flesh and blood, but the spiritual powers of darkness. You must remember this wisdom because God's enemies hate His children, who will displace them. Unlike most of those children, you're aware of the battle in spiritual realms, and that makes you dangerous. You will be victorious, but there will be a personal cost for the conquest. Never forget that the price is worth paying."

When my grandmother's hand reached for mine, a measure of the strength she once had seemed to be revived. The veins under her papery, warm skin reminded me of strong, nourishing roots, and I imagined this hand wielding unlikely weapons against the enemies she was referring to. She announced, "You, my child, are a descendant in the bloodline of the Ellisons, and you walk here on earth with the Creator and Savior of the world!"

Spellbound, as if I never heard these words before, I kept my eyes locked on hers. The future is not mine to foresee, but with this assurance, I can face it. By His power, I can do the work Christ called me to when He put me here, for such a time as this.

My grandmother's eyes softened, and she smiled. I wondered if Christ might send a like-minded spouse or friend into my life to create a pair, like the bulbs in her braided twine cords. She was blessed with my grandfather, and it was their leather case with the silver clasp that my father carried with him tonight. Someday, the family Bible might have another entry, carefully penned in ink. But until then, I will face life with the help that is provided.

My grandmother's roads are now in the past, and I am not likely to walk them. But she warned me about an enemy that is not limited to space or time until Jesus returns. She has prepared me for my own encounters because I am entrusted with a legacy of power, strength, and wisdom.

I am Mercedes Ellison, and I cannot escape my destiny.

Putting down the journal, Mercedes went to her bathroom to grab some tissues. The words she had read spoke to her doubts, her efforts to escape a legacy that cost her and her family so much. The teenager in the journal counted it a privilege to be an Ellison and to become a faithful, battle-scarred follower of Christ.

She wiped away tears, shaken by the conviction of her ancestors. It would be a restless night.

Chapter 2

Zach Boone stood in the shade of an awning over the apartment mail station on his university campus in Virginia, anticipating an envelope from Lenoir Bassett and Madigan, PC. It was on top, and he quickly tore open the seal. As he expected, an expensive vellum invitation congratulated him again and invited him to attend a company celebration for new members. They were looking forward to meeting his guest, reminding him to bring his girlfriend to the event on the firm's property on Hilton Head Island, South Carolina.

"Yes!" he breathed, grabbing the remaining letters, and closing the box. He flipped through, sorting, and tossing junk mail into the nearby trash container. An envelope with a South Carolina postmark and no return address aroused his curiosity, so he opened it next. Taken aback at the message typed on the plain white paper, he read it again.

Lenoir Bassett and Madigan, P.C. is under investigation for serious crimes. Distance yourself from signing on with the firm and do not get Mercedes Ellison involved. -A friend.

Zach scowled, scrutinizing his surroundings. There was nothing suspicious in the crowds of students and the windows of buildings and vehicles nearby, but he was uncomfortable. He swiftly refolded the letter and jogged toward his apartment with the rest of his mail.

"Mr. Boone opened and read the warning," reported a dark-haired young man as he watched Zach Boone rush off with his mail. "He's suspicious and looking around."

"Zach wouldn't know you if he saw you," came the mature voice on the cell phone. "It was right to warn him. He's fortunate that you're on board, or he'd be on his own."

The young man sighed and wiped a hand over his face. "You know why I'm nervous. Mercedes could be in grave danger, and Zach is oblivious. He believes he got this job on his own merit. Do you know how long it takes to graduate from law school, and how much it cost?"

"That's why he will ignore the warning and take the job. We'll see what kind of man he is. There's nothing more you can do up there. Drive back and we'll discuss some additional evidence that just came in."

The young man ended the call with his employer on the business cell phone and dropped it in the cup holder of the rental car he sat in. In his wildest dreams, he never imagined his role as former archaeologist who began working with antiquities would bring him to this.

Reaching for a tote bag stuffed to overflowing, Mercedes' new landlady waved a hand dismissively at her formal greeting and laughed. "Just call me Lois," she said. "I've known your mother's family for ages, and there are no finer people. We'll be good friends."

Lois dressed in gardening attire that had not yet been in the dirt this morning, and she led Mercedes from the brick paved driveway to an enchanting flagstone path, chatting along the way. "You'll fit right in here in Bluffton with that Jeep, you know. That teal color is adorable! Folks 'round here love their recreational vehicles and do a lot of biking, kayaking, hiking, boating, fishing, and beach lovin'. You'll need to get some decals to personalize the back to entertain everyone on the road at traffic lights. Someone here today will get that kayak and bike unloaded for you. The storage shed is in the garden."

"Thank you, Lois. Recreation is one reason I have it, but my work sometimes takes me into abandoned places where roads aren't good. My dad wanted me to have a vehicle rugged enough to keep me from getting stranded."

Lois fiddled with keys until she pushed open the door of the cottage. Then she handed a keyring with a bright sunflower charm on it to Mercedes. "This set is yours, dear, and it includes one for the storage building," Lois told her. "You can stash things out of the way in there, just keep them in the area marked for the cottage."

Mercedes put her purse and laptop bag down on the quartz countertop of a kitchen island, gazing around the apartment. "Oh, Lois, this is better in person than in the photos. It's so airy! I'm blessed that you were ready to rent."

Her landlady beamed as she looked around. "It's been a satisfying challenge. I'm glad someone like you is the first tenant. Someday, I hope to lure my granddaughter back to town to live in it. Bluffton wasn't big enough for her, so she took a job up in Charlotte. But now she sees the city life isn't the answer she was lookin' for."

The wistful look in Lois' eyes evaporated when she turned to Mercedes. "Go on and look around the place. It's fully furnished, and I equipped the kitchen with the basics. The French doors open to the pool, garden, and courtyard. As you saw on the contract, because you paid in advance for the summer, weekly housekeeping is included. I'll get Aaron to unload for you, then we'll show you around the grounds."

Setting the last bag of groceries on the counter, Mercedes quickly reached into her purse for her ringing cellphone. She smiled to see Zach's picture on the screen. "Hi, Zach!"

"Hi, Babe, how's the cottage?"

"It's amazing—I'll love it here this summer! I hope our schedules work out so you can stop by to see it."

Mercedes held the phone to her ear with one hand and reached into a grocery bag with the other, pulling out things for the freezer before they thawed. "About that," Zach said. "I'll be riding through late tonight, but I'm expected at the beach property where I'll be staying. It looks like I'm stuck in some meetings and training with the company for a few days at a conference center on the island, but we'll end with a celebration over the weekend. They told me to be sure and invite you."

She sighed and walked to the French doors overlooking the pool and garden. "Zach, you know I don't attend parties where people are drinking. I know a few things 'cause I've seen a few things."

"And normally, I agree with you. It's worse that they're mixing alcohol with business. But this company really wants young men with wives or who are seriously committed to a relationship. They consider you part of the package and this is important to me, Mercedes. Please, please come down on Friday evening. We'll make an appearance and get away quickly, maybe make some excuse about a walk on the beach to catch up on time alone together. They have a double room set aside for you and Jana, Declan's girlfriend. She doesn't drink, either. The list of things she doesn't do is a mile longer than the ones she does."

The sarcasm in his voice made Mercedes pause. Did he talk to others about her the same way he talked about Jana? He clearly ignored their principles for compromise, if it was to his own benefit, and expected Mercedes to do the same—for his benefit.

She doused a flash of anger and decided she would wait to mention his selfishness. He was in a rush, and she didn't feel like arguing, anyway. "I can give you a solid 'I'll think about it.'"

Zach's voice grew huskier. "Baby, this isn't just about me, you know. This is for us. I think you know what's next if everything goes well this week."

"It's been almost six weeks since we spent time together in person, Zach. We have things to talk about. I can be on the island sometime this weekend without staying there."

"I'm texting you the address for the beach house. They scattered the firm into two of them, built beside one another. They aren't in a gated community, but they are back off the road, so look for the bricked column mailbox. And I'm adding Jana's cell number. Call her. She's got some of your same food issues and ideas about how you two can plan. I've got to get on the road now. Declan and Jana are waiting."

As they ended their call, Mercedes slowly put her cellphone down on the countertop, where an iridescent shimmer caught the light and raced it through veins of pale aqua and gray in the white quartz. Idly, she traced the shimmering abstraction with a fingertip. A year ago, she'd been excited to be asked out by Zach after being introduced to him at a conference for young professionals. She was starting out as an independent architectural historian, and he was meeting representatives of firms that were hiring upcoming graduates from law school.

He was just what she needed, a guy who was logical, practical, and eager. Things were simple with Zach. He wanted to solve problems as a litigation lawyer. Every day would be different. He would have a variety of cases to challenge his negotiating skills, and none were likely to go as far as a trial in a courtroom.

But her relationship with Zach now was like a balloon with a slow leak. Unless he did something dramatic soon to revive it, it would end.

Mercedes sighed and turned to put the rest of her groceries in the pantry, trying to shake off a familiar unease that grew in her spirit. Something was off about this job that Zach wanted so much. Last night, the journal entry she read raised questions about her decision to run from the occasional intuitive events that popped up in her life, scary and unbidden, usually with a personal cost. This might be one time she should pay attention.

She spent the rest of the evening listening to soothing music and settling into the cottage. In her dreams later that night, she ran along an iridescent shimmer by an aqua stream with banks of pearly gray sand. The path was irresistible, but she did not know where it led. Suddenly, muscular arms she must have been running toward embraced her, and the shimmer spread over vast sand dunes, creating a mirage that danced over the baking sand. She was on an archaeological site where she once served as an intern. Then she looked up at the person whose arms held her, a familiar face in shadows created by the shady shelter under his Panama hat.

Mercedes gasped, sitting up in bed, shaking off sleep and sweating as if she had been back in Egypt.

The following morning, Mercedes texted her mother before a lunch meeting with the client she had in Bluffton. *I sent you an email with attachments to you earlier this morning. Did you get them?*

Yes. Fascinating and disturbing, all at once. Your dad will be back home this afternoon, and I'll show him. He'll probably call the Holmwoods to help do the research you're asking about. You must have been reading the journal again last night. Is it upsetting you?

Her heart leaped and unexpected tears stung her eyes. She gulped and typed. *Yes.*

Can I call?

Tonight. I'll be with a historic preservation committee all afternoon. I'll let you know.

Love you!

Texting a heart emoji and putting her phone into a silky lined pocket of her purse, Mercedes took the flagstone path to the brick paver driveway. A white car crept by. She wasn't close enough to see the driver through tinted windows and there was nothing special to draw her attention, but her intuition peaked.

Lunch with her clients was relaxed and in the open air at a local restaurant. After her travels for vacation, study, and work in other places, she valued the unique flavor of life that was the Lowcountry. She thought of home as being on "island time" and kept flexible schedules. The gracious standard of living in the Lowcountry was about being all there to enjoy a moment.

Property tours rounded out her afternoon. Leaving for the day, she stepped carefully over a mosaic of concrete sidewalk broken by the roots of an ancient oak. When she looked back up, the white car that drove past Lois' driveway was parallel parked nearby in a marked space on Calhoun Street.

Mercedes paused and adjusted the shoulder strap of her laptop bag, pretending to look over the signs of homey small businesses along the street. Her sunglasses hid her eyes, which were evaluating her escape route.

Pretending to decide about where to shop, she strolled up some sun-splashed, creaky wooden steps to a generous porch and entered a welcoming, approachable art gallery. She kept a respectable distance near several other guests, all of them enjoying and commenting on Lowcountry themed paintings and sculpture. When the attendant on duty began a friendly exchange about one painting with a couple of tourists, Mercedes ducked out an open back door to a path that led to a sandy parking area and the next street.

The white sedan was nowhere in sight as she pushed the button to start her Jeep, and she saw no one hanging around. If she was being watched, her diversion worked, and she breathed a prayer of thanks. Then she asked Jesus for special protection and discernment about being followed. Was she simply edgy today? She felt no threat or dread, only that something was unusual about the car. Keeping her focus on situational awareness, Mercedes drove a few blocks away to the summer cottage.

Aaron, the contractor working at her landlady's house, was getting out of his pickup with a grocery bag when Mercedes slid her Jeep into her parking spot. He raked his cap back over his mostly white hair to tidy it, then waved and hailed her from his open door. He stood waiting on the flagstone path.

"Miss Ellison, I went to my friend's dock for fresh fish," he announced in a rich local accent. "I asked Miss Lois if I could grill them here for both of you. See, I'm a bachelor, and fish is best while it's hot."

"Oh, Aaron, that sounds wonderful! I love fish, but I don't eat shellfish. I have a few food intolerances and allergies, but Lois knows what they are. Can I help?"

He raised the bag with a deeply tanned arm. "I've got everything it takes for decent salad bar and Lois is bakin' potatoes. If you have anything special you need for those, bring it along. Say, forty-five minutes?"

Mercedes agreed and made her way to the cottage to put away her business things and change clothes. She went to the refrigerator for her favorite salad dressing and ingredients to make a quick allergy-friendly tartar sauce. With minutes to spare, she texted her mom that she was having dinner with Lois but would check in afterwards.

Through the French doors, she saw Aaron and Lois setting the patio table. She paused, seeing these two senior citizens working together, acting more like close friends or a couple than a business relationship. She quickly carried her contributions to the meal out the doors and greeted them, then she busied herself with helping. The conversation was so easy and her hosts so engaging that it was only as she sat with them in the rosy glow of sunset that Mercedes remembered something she wanted to ask them.

"Lois does one of your neighbors drive a late model white sedan?" she ventured.

Her landlady was thoughtful for a few moments. "Not that I know of, but someone may have a new car. There's another house on the street with a recently renovated carriage house apartment, and they may have guests. Have you noticed, Aaron?"

The contractor scowled with concentration, which deepened the lifetime of wrinkles on his face. He scratched a day's graying stubble on his chin and slowly shook his head. "No, but I haven't paid attention. Tourists are a fact of life. None of the neighbors have a car like that. Know the model?"

"I'm afraid the selection of sedans on the roads is a blur for me, but I'll try to notice the emblem on the front of this one if it shows up again. I couldn't see the tag information. It could be an out-of-state tourist."

Aaron cleared his throat and peered into her eyes. "Is someone botherin' you?"

She withered under the curiosity of the two older friends. "Oh—no, I just—it drove by the driveway slowly this morning as I left, then I saw it parked near where my meeting was this afternoon. I feel foolish for mentioning it."

Lois studied her, then asked, "Is your intuition naggin' at you when you see that car, Mercedes?"

Mercedes squeezed her eyes shut and nodded. She opened them again to meet Lois' solemn gaze.

The older woman solemnly said, "Don't ignore your gut reactions to things like that, even if it makes no sense. Pay attention to your discernment."

After a call with her parents, Mercedes went to bed with her phone to answer texts before turning out the lights. The first one was from Jana. She would be flexible tomorrow to connect with Jana about the weekend. Then she opened the text from Zach.

Meetings all day and I'm on my way out to dinner. I wish I had time to call. Can't wait to see you here on Friday! Did you reach Jana about plans for the weekend?

With an irritated sigh, Mercedes turned off her phone and set it on the nightstand charger.

Chapter 3

"You're a Christian, right? I mean, a real one, somebody who's born again and tries to live what the Bible teaches," asked Jana.

Taken aback at this question right off the bat after exchanging hellos, Mercedes cautiously replied, "Yes." Eyeing her cellphone screen in a stand that allowed her to use the speaker, she idly rolled her ink pen in her hand, anticipating an interesting conversation.

Jana heaved a sigh. "I'm a Christian, too," she said. "This place feels all wrong. I can't explain it and I know how this must sound, but if you don't come tomorrow for the weekend, can I drive up and stay with you until Declan is done at the beach house? I'm done with him by then if this keeps up. He and Zach are acting weird, talking about how their number has given them a new insight into who they really are and the freedom to maximize their lives for their roles in the law firm."

Mercedes sat bolt upright. "Their *number*?"

"Yeah, their training yesterday included a personality test, and they brought back books to read to learn how to act on the results," Jana replied. "If they sign on with the firm, they will attend routine group meetings on how their numbers work with their team. I couldn't sleep last night after looking up info on those books with my laptop."

Mercedes asked Jana if the books used a specific terminology designed similarly to a pentagram for the personality categories.

"Yes! Do you know anything about that?" Jana exclaimed.

Mercedes shot up to her feet, dropped her pen and notepad on the coffee table in disgust, and muttered, "I can't believe it!"

"Believe it. My research tells me that this baloney is full of New Age mysticism, a path to higher states of being, essence and enlightenment, like being one with God. I don't know about your Bible, but mine teaches that the only true God is on His throne, and He won't share it. Christianity is never about looking inward except to examine our hearts and confess sin. We become new creations when we accept Him, and He allows no excuses for sin because we believe we were born with a certain personality. He saves us from ourselves. Christianity is about looking to Jesus and surrendering our lives to serve Him."

Jana stopped to catch her breath, then said, "I'm sorry, Mercedes. I didn't mean to preach a sermon. I'm just worked up and haven't slept much."

Pacing in front of the coffee table now, Mercedes said, "The first sin in the Bible was when God's adversary promised Eve equality with God, and she went for it. The inventor of these teachings admitted to making them up via channeling, which is when an influencing spirit takes over in automatic writing."

"I know! Oh, I'm so relieved you understand what I'm up against—what we are up against. It's no coincidence that you are here right now. I'm surrounded by people pickled in themselves down here."

"Yes, self-realization is a preoccupation with oneself, which is rooted in rebellion, which the book of 1 Samuel calls witchcraft."

Bible verses flooded her mind, and she had to turn back to her phone speaker to give Jana her attention. Jana was saying,

"Two guys brought their wives along and this morning, I saw a book one of them carried. My skin furred up at the topic, a course about miracles."

"That one was written by channeling spirits, too, back in the 1970s. It's full of things people want to believe, Jana, and promoted by daytime talk show queens with book clubs, so it's difficult to have a dissenting conversation about it. Unless we know our Bible, in context, these teachings can mislead the best of us."

"I love Declan, but I absolutely will not stick around if he adopts this in his life," said Jana. "Like the Bible says, what has light to do with darkness? What will you do, Mercedes?"

Mercedes tried to rub away the tension in her temples, where a headache was coming on. "Jana, I need to pray and think. Can I call you back later this afternoon?"

Mercedes closed her laptop with a snap. She was too shaken to fill out reports for work and there was no looming deadline to finish.

With her hands wrapped around the comforting warmth of her cup of ginger tea, she sat back on the sofa cushions and started praying for guidance about how best to handle the situation she found herself in. Jana was waiting, and a lot was at stake.

Her phone vibrated with a text notification in the stand where she left it, and she glanced to see if it was urgent enough for the interruption.

It was her Bible Study leader, checking in on her to see how she was doing in her summer cottage. Only a handful of her group were in town for the season, so they agreed to keep tabs on each other and share prayers.

Was this text an instant answer to prayer? This was someone with a solid foundation in scripture and a godly track record of faith.

Mercedes typed quickly to reply. *The cottage is amazing, and you'd love my landlady. The job mostly involves a lot of records and forms to file. But some sudden challenges have popped up in my life. One of those is that a new Christian friend needs immediate help to talk about E-grams, with her boyfriend and Zach. Zach's new job required the test in training. I dread dealing with this. I could use some advice and prayer.*

She sipped her tea as she waited. Her Bible Study leader responded. *I wish I could call you, but I'm on a break from work. When you researched this issue and helped friends navigate through it with other friends, you didn't think you'd go unscathed by it, did you? Jesus prepared you for such a time as this. Don't let Zach grill you with his attorney's techniques and don't argue. Catch him in his own trap with the contradictions he must face. You are about to discover if he's really a believer. Make him prove his case against the Bible. You both do research for a living. Ask for data, primary sources, context, and coherence.*

Mercedes groaned, inwardly cringing at the prospect of confrontation, then she found a stressed-out emoticon to use in her text before she typed her answer. *I'm not adequate for this! People are ready to die on this hill to defend those things.*

Her teacher responded. *Are you refusing to engage in this obvious opportunity to serve Jesus? Who benefits from that?*

Seconds ticked by as this question speared Mercedes' soul. She and Jana had just been preaching to each other that

Christians don't focus on themselves, but on living for Jesus. He equips His people with what they need for the task set before them, regardless of whether they identify with it in their personality type.

Her texted response was a commitment. *If that was a battle-cry, it worked. Thank you for the attitude change and the advice. Cover me in prayer for the next few days.*

I always do.

Mercedes opened a notebook and started jotting down the tumble of things in her mind. Then, she picked up her Bible from the sofa end table to look up some verses she recalled, and searched topics online for the ones she had forgotten.

Something her Great-Great Grand Aunt had written in her journal about the garlic braid kept nagging at her mind. *I will face life with the help that is provided... I am Mercedes Ellison, and I cannot escape my destiny.*

Tears stung her eyes, and she reached for her cellphone to text Jana again. *Hi Jana, when you are free, please call me. I'll come down and stay at the beach house tomorrow night, and we'll see what Saturday brings, if Zach and I are still a couple. I was just doing Bible Study on the issue you told me about earlier, and I will do more on the topic tonight. Are you open to discussing this with Declan and Zach together as a group? My thinking is, you and I are like-minded, and we are stronger together. Having the Holy Spirit with us makes a three-fold cord that can't be broken. I was reading some verses like Ecclesiastes 4:9-12 and Mark 6:7. There are others, plus the ones about the practice of having two witnesses.*

After Jana called, Mercedes packed some groceries for meals to suit their special diets. She packed a small suitcase for a weekend at the law firm's beach house, but she expected to be back at the cottage on Saturday. There would be no reason to stay.

Lois or Aaron had left a local community paper on her doormat that morning, and she glanced over it while waiting on the air fryer timer for her dinner to be ready. On the front page, her attention was arrested by a large photo of a dolphin playing near swimmers. Another one played shyly behind it. The article headline proclaimed that a marine biologist living on Hilton Head Island had been swimming alongside friendly dolphins that were coming close to shore and playfully teasing swimmers and beach walkers with their antics. One young dolphin was coming closer and getting bolder. Some residents were throwing around the idea of a contest for naming it, and others considered adopting it as a mascot.

The timer announced dinner was ready, and Mercedes folded the small paper and set it aside. She was hungry, and the news about the dolphin put her in the mood to swim tonight. Doing some laps in the pool would be a great tension reliever.

Zach Boone went down the hall of the two-story beach house to meet the group for dinner out together again. He was early, but there was nothing to do in his room while Declan showered. The living area should be quiet enough to get in a phone call or text conversation with Mercedes. There was no response from her after his last one, but Declan told him she had been in touch with Jana.

So much was going on in his head from the training and presentations of the last two days that he had little time to think of her. But as he showered and dressed for the evening, he felt a pang of loneliness.

A voice hailed him as he passed the open door of the room used as an office and library. Mr. Lenoir's attractive secretary invited him in and told him to drop the formalities of the training sessions and call her Jill. They exchanged pleasantries, and he said he was looking forward to meeting Mr. Lenoir when he arrived for the weekend.

"He will be excited to meet you, as well. What time will your girlfriend be here?"

The question caught him off guard. "Well—I'm not sure. I haven't had time to call her. The firm is keeping me busy right now," he replied, flashing his most disarming smile. If Jill had a bad side, it was out of sight, and he didn't want to be on it.

She returned the smile, and he waited while she eyed him. He knew this look, and he drew a deep breath.

"Well, she must show up while Mr. Lenoir is here," she said, and slowly came around the desk to stand before him. "But you're free tonight. Will you play the knight in shining armor and sit with me at dinner?"

The young woman snaked her slender arm through his as they went to the living area, where others involved in the training sessions were gathering. Delcan blinked in shock, opening his mouth, but he quickly snapped it back shut. His eyes communicated confusion and then a warning.

At dinner, while the conversations at the table were getting more boisterous with shared personal stories, Zach leaned closer to the secretary and kept his voice low. "So, tell me why my girlfriend must meet Mr. Lenoir this weekend."

Jill gave him a knowing smile, waving at the server to fill their wine glasses again. When he moved on, she kept her voice low and sultry. "She's the reason you are being hired."

Zach scowled. "No, I was in consideration right before I met her, when I built the best hypothetical case for the firm's graduate contest topic. I won the top points for it."

An employee hailed her a few seats down to confirm an account of the bizarre behavior of a former client. Everyone laughed at the story, but Zach pasted a distracted smile on his face. The beauty at his side saw his expression as she turned to him, then she put her hand on his sleeve and leaned closer. "Even when your girlfriend becomes your wife, she won't be an obstacle."

Startled, Zach blinked, then took a gulp from his glass. He needed more wine to forget the note in his mailbox warning him not to get Mercedes Ellison involved in his association with Lenoir Bassett and Madigan, P.C.

A grove of lanky pines breathed and whispered over a suntanned, well-built young man who strolled slowly down the street in front of Lois' house in Old Town Bluffton. He wore a ball cap with a history blog logo and designer sunglasses, and he held his cellphone to his ear. In his other hand was a dazzling lavender leash that linked him to a boutique dog breed he couldn't pronounce. The pet looked like a silly stuffed animal. A small pink bag for dog waste hung through the belt of his shorts.

"If she left the house, she walked. The Jeep was in the driveway all day. Maybe she won't go down to the island. They could have more privacy if Zach drove up here for the afternoon."

He herded the dog back from an interesting smell at the base of a traffic sign while the man on the other side of the conversation snorted. "I just left the restaurant where the firm's employees are enjoying an expensive dinner out, and our boy Zach is sharing some wine as he gets to know Mr. Lenoir's secretary a lot better. He doesn't want to leave the beach party."

"Oh." The antiquities investigator considered this news as he picked up the tiny dog to keep from jerking the designer leash. Then he turned to walk back down the street and said sharply, "He could have spared her all this! He's using Mercedes Ellison because she makes him look good. Don't worry, I'll watch to see if she leaves tomorrow, though I'm not sure how. She's on to me in the car."

The other man whistled. "That good, huh?"

Setting the little animal gently back on the weathered old sidewalk away from the sign, the investigator said impatiently, "Yes, she's that good. I warned you. Today, I had to jog twice, bike, and offer to walk an elderly woman's ridiculous dog several times to keep surveillance on the driveway. It will be impossible for me to tail Miss Ellison in that car without being noticed, and she may even know who I am by now."

"Well, no matter. I've got informants as housekeeping staff embedded in the beach houses. I'll know if she arrives. Scope out the public beach access located beside the house. There's a parking area there, and she's not likely to take the trouble to look for the car."

Following the blur of trotting pixie steps by the bejeweled pooch in the pink glow of fading daylight, the investigator gave his hat an agitated tug. "All right. Remember, my report isn't legal if I trespass. When Lenoir gets in your jurisdiction, the rest is on you."

Pink and gold light flushed over the courtyard and pool in front of the cottage when Mercedes came out through the French doors. The tiled pavers were warm on her bare feet as she slipped out of her cover-up and draped it on the closest lounge chair. Lights in the pool were just coming on, creating an aqua neon glow that reminded her of the sea around the Florida Keys.

Mildly cool and silky water slid over her as she swam idly along in the tranquil turquoise. She wondered if this was what it was like to swim with a friendly bottlenose dolphin, like the one in the local news, whose slippery skin looked like satin. Her stress and strain dissolved, as did the resistance to what she would face tomorrow, and her concern over inevitable endings.

Exhausted ripples slapped the sides of the pool as she rose on the tiered steps. Darkness fled from the cheerful twinkle of brass lanterns around the courtyard and insects sang their evening anthems in the murky shadows of semi-tropical plants and palms on the edge of the property.

With a contented sigh, she stretched out on the lounge chair to drip dry. Somewhere in the twilight between wakefulness and sleeping, water that was clear, yet turquoise, slid over her body deliciously. She felt only peace and joy as she glided along, and then a surge of excitement when muscular arms encircled her to pull her under. Sputtering, she broke the surface, then laughed. Before her was the suntanned face she loved and would never forget. His dark hair clung to his forehead in dripping clumps and his blue eyes were at once both arresting and gentle.

Mercedes stirred and sat up. She gave herself the few moments she knew it would take for the bittersweet memory to dissipate and her heart to stop aching. It was time to go inside, for she should text Zach about her plans to drive down to the island tomorrow.

Chapter 4

Water sparkled like glitter under the causeway bridge as Mercedes crossed it, driving the few minutes it took from Bluffton to Hilton Head Island. Sails stirred the cloudless blue sky and sea birds pecked through tasty morsels along the marshy banks. She passed Pinkney Island Wildlife Refuge and breathed a deep sigh of anticipation. Soon, she would pack her cruiser bicycle and come to explore the trails there.

Her phone media connection drew her attention from breathtaking views. A Christian worldview podcast was coming on, and after introductions, the guest speaker answered a question with a quote. "Well, as C. S. Lewis once said, look for yourself and you will find in the long run only hatred, loneliness, despair, rage, ruin, and decay. But look for Christ, and you will find Him, and with Him, everything else thrown on. We should ask ourselves; do we really believe God is sufficient? We cannot isolate this from our worldview."

The host and guest went on with the interview, but Mercedes whispered a prayer. "Jesus, you are sufficient. I can't see what lies ahead and don't know what to do, and I feel on the edge of something life changing. Keep me in Your will."

Mercedes accidentally passed the brick column with a mailbox and numbers Zach had given her, so she explored a little further down the side road to find a good place to turn around. Part of the charm about Hilton Head Island was that once she was off the beaten path, the threading roads and trails engulfed her in nature. She passed a road and signs for a boat dock for residents only. Soon, she came to a circle and rounded it to go back toward the drive for the beach houses.

She slowed for bicycles near the entrance after she made the turn around. A small cart pulled by a young father held a sleeping infant and another pulled behind the mother's bike carried the family dog. Three children of varying ages rode along with them. All wore smiles and waved at her.

In the afterglow of the family's joy and the way they shared it with her, she was still smiling when she turned into the crushed shell trail driveway that led to the pair of beach houses. The setting was lovely, and someone clearly designed it with care for the natural surroundings. It was the kind of place lots of money and good taste could build.

Mercedes pulled up to the second house, where Jana had told her to park beside Declan's SUV. But a young woman with a stylish short hairstyle came out the front doors and waved at her to stop. She came to Mercedes' window.

Breathless, she announced, "Hi, Mercedes! I'm Jana. Do you mind if we go out somewhere for lunch? I'll take your cooler in and put things in the fridge, then I'll be out in a flash."

Bemused, Mercedes laughed and agreed. She put the Jeep in park with the engine running, then helped Jana find the cooler in the back. The nonperishables would be fine until they returned.

She pulled around in the circle driveway and had the side door unlocked when Jana rushed out. Her pretty passenger turned to her with a sheepish grin. "I didn't mean to accost you and impose, but I can't take that place another minute. If you weren't here, I'd have driven Declan's car to the beach shops to get away."

Mercedes waved her hand dismissively while she studied her new friend. "Oh, it's not an imposition at all! I love the idea of going out for lunch! But I'm curious, can you explain why this house bothers you so much? I'm an architectural historian and deal with a lot of buildings and property, some of which I would describe as creepy. So, to me, you don't sound nutty. Many people are sensitive to a particular—"

She paused, searching for a safe word. "*Atmosphere,* one peculiar to the personality of a place."

Jana stared wide-eyed for a second before she burst out laughing, bent over in the seat. Mercedes started laughing, too, and by the time they stopped, both dabbed at tears in their eyes. Mercedes reached behind her seat for tissues and took one, then handed the box to Jana.

Her passenger took a deep breath to settle down, then turned a wan smile at Mercedes. "Just say it—some people can sense spirits in a place, something that lingers there, like a territory. They aren't ghosts of dead folks, that's not real. The entities I'm referring to can also accompany a person who comes around. I sense things like that, and I'm undecided about whether it's a blessing or a curse. I prayed over my room, and it feels okay, but other places in there are like you described it—creepy."

Someone pulled a curtain back at a window in the house and then quickly let go. Mercedes narrowed her eyes, waiting, but there was only a reflection of a nearby sago palm on the glass.

She eased out toward the road. "Do you know much about the history of the island? There were once some spiritually deceptive traditions around here that might linger, as you say, in places that were once marsh and woods. Vacation homes and resorts are there now. I'm not suggesting this is troubling you about the beach house, but you seem to have a solid understanding about it and should consider it."

"No, I've heard nothing at all about the island, except that some Illuminati-types sometimes gather here to plan how to rule and destroy the world."

Mercedes laughed and waited on some light traffic on the road before turning. She was really going to enjoy time spent with this vivacious new friend. "You'll find references to that sort of thing in island history, especially if you know the names to watch out for. But I learned other disturbing things about more down-to-earth residents at the local history museum. By the way, do you have a place in mind for lunch? If not, I know some great ones, right on the water at Skull Creek where the fishing boats dock."

"*Skull* Creek? Are you serious?" squeaked Jana. She lightly slapped her face. "I might have known. Okay, no matter how bad that sounds, I trust you. Take me anywhere that serves great seafood and then tell me about the disturbing local things you know about. I'm in the right mood for that."

When she stopped laughing at Jana's reaction, Mercedes told her about how, until the modern era, church communities were an important part of island life. Children aged twelve to thirteen went into the woods seeking a religious experience. A church elder would accompany the child and evaluate the child's dreams or visions and interpret their meanings. "Once the child had an experience like this, he or she could then return to the community congregation to recite them," she told Jana. "Afterwards, church membership was affirmed."

Stunned, Jana sat staring at Mercedes while she pulled into a sandy restaurant parking lot. "But this invites invented stories! Imagine the pressure on those kids to measure up to the others who were affirmed. Besides, we're never told in Scripture to go looking for a spiritual vision to prove we are fit to belong to a body of believers, but we *are* told that it is nobler to believe without signs and wonders."

Mercedes nodded, sitting back to talk, leaving the air conditioning on. "Right, there's a lot that wasn't biblical about their beliefs, yet is this really much different from what we see all around us in churches today? That's been on my mind lately, and I'm studying about bringing 'strange fire' into worship, you know, slapping a label of 'Christian' on a pagan practice and including it in a church as if it's legitimate. Here's another belief they had. If you see colored glass bottles hanging from trees or stuck on fake decorative trees around here, this was a tradition rooted in the entrapment of evil spirits who sneak around houses at night. This is also why 'haint blue' is a popular color for porch ceilings, doors, and shutters here in the South, especially the Lowcountry. They believed it confused the evil spirits, which completely underestimates the intelligence of evil beings. We are not on their level of power and can't trick them."

"So, they believed in evil spirits?"

"Extremely so, and that makes them smarter and more in tune with the spiritual reality of our faith than most modern Christians. They understood that humanity is in the invisible battle between God and evil beings. They just misinterpreted how to live with that reality, probably mixing it with other traditions. The Holy Spirit in our hearts trumps any adversary, so we don't need charms and traps to ward off evil. I was in the local museum when I read about the children being required to experience a spiritual encounter, and after a chill ran over me, my first thought was that this was incredibly dangerous. We should never seek a spirit, for it invites deception by an evil entity. The Holy Spirit isn't ours to command, for enlightenment or our personal gain. He is God, not our magic genie."

A hostess with a perky ponytail seated Mercedes and Jana at a table with a fabulous view of the long dock. Screaming sea gulls and splashing dolphins escorted an incoming fishing boat on Skull Creek. The restaurant menus were like the rustic table, homey but clean, and deciding what to order was no simple task, given their allergy limitations. They ordered a salad with blackened fish and shared several other vegetable dishes to try something new.

As they waited for lunch, Jana took a sip of sweet tea and then said, "You're not what I expected, Mercedes. You're like fresh air and sunshine. It's not just the long blonde hair that threw me. You have a presence about you. When I heard your name, I expected you to have a dark-haired European look, brooding and sultry. You seemed so grounded on the phone, like—I don't know, like someone with authority. Then when I saw you, I immediately thought of a cheerleader! Such a contradiction."

Mercedes laughed, accustomed to dealing with surprise about her name. She sipped some fresh lemonade, then replied, "It's okay, I get that. I'm named for my Great-Great Grand Aunt, and her mother was Spanish, but there are plenty of blondes in Spain. It's also a French name, so people I meet sometimes think I should look French. From family portraits and descriptions, I'm told I look like my namesake's grandmother, Claire. Same hair, same eyes, same—"

She stopped short, unwilling to share so much about herself with someone she had just met. With a small shrug, she said, "Enough about me. Tell me about yourself. Did you go to college with Declan and Zach?"

"Oh, no, I met Declan at a singles event at church about six months ago. I have a bachelor's degree in business, so we were in different educational circles. When Zach attends church, it's just for worship services, not Bible studies or groups."

A young man came to their table balancing a platter of food, warning them about which dishes were hot to the touch as he set them down. Jana offered to say grace over the enticing aromas on the table, then they selected items to try for their own plates.

Along with her food, Mercedes digested the nugget of information about Zach's commitment to church. He never willingly talked about his faith and avoided any deep conversations about the Bible, but he said he was a Christian and could recall the day he committed his life and salvation to Jesus. She had planned to give him the benefit of the doubt until he graduated, knowing he was under a lot of pressure to study. He was in school in Virginia when they met about a year ago, so they texted often, had video calls, and arranged a date every other month to go out somewhere.

"Hello," Jana said gently, waving her fork before Mercedes' face. She grinned when Mercedes blushed.

"Sorry. You were saying?"

"I wasn't saying anything, but I will now. What attracts you to Zach, besides the obvious? Few guys are so handsome or carry themselves so well. And he has manners, a man who won't embarrass a well-bred girl."

Mercedes smiled and took a swallow of her lemonade. "He's cool, logical, and analytical. He has lofty goals and the drive to work for them. Some women don't know how to appreciate that. They want men to live for them, to chase and handle them, to get all tangled in emotions and waste life in tempests in teapots. It gives them power over men who think with something other than brains."

Jana blinked her lovely brown eyes in surprise and burst out laughing, sitting back in her chair. People at nearby tables glanced at them and smiled.

"Maybe that's why you've lasted so long with him," Jana said. "Declan told me Zach gets chased and has dated often, but he rarely sees the same woman more than twice."

"Oh, that's easily explained. He will drop any woman who pressures him to make her the focus of his life. Emotionally needy people irritate him and disrupt his goals. I believe he wants commitment, but only after he proves something to himself. Is Declan like that?"

Jana shook her head and laughed. "No, he's warm and personable, funny, and loyal almost to a fault. But like Zach, he won't marry until he settles into a career. He also won't marry a woman who isn't a Christian, and those are hard to find. Declan tells me that men these days have given up on women. From their point of view, they feel demeaned and scorned by the feminist influence and they refuse to marry and get taken for a ride financially when it ends in divorce. Most marriages end that way. I can't say I blame them, but what's going to become of a culture where there is no core family unit?"

Mercedes looked out over the water, watching gulls and herons scout for fish. "It falls. Destroying marriage and the family unit directly violates God's original plan for us. And that's precisely why it's under attack."

As they pulled into the beach house driveway again, Jana sighed and became restless as a hen, running her fingers through her short, dark hair. She turned away from the house, looking into the landscape of palms and exotic plants against a backdrop of pine groves.

Mercedes pursed her lips and felt a flutter in her stomach. The reprieve to enjoy lunch with a like-minded sister in Christ had boosted her spirits and melded them together into the strength of a team, but trouble with a capital T had not magically gone away.

She entered the front door with her suitcase and Jana, who was now subdued as she toted a few other things from the Jeep. Mercedes found the house large, open, and airy. She waited for her own unjaded impressions about it, and had to admit it felt close, as if she walked into dark paneled walls and austere family portraits.

Once inside their shared accommodations, they plopped Mercedes' bags on one bed. It was a comfortable room, not fussed over, and the owners decorated it in a casual coastal theme. Unusual seashells filled a clear sculpted dish on the nightstand between their beds.

Jana hung a few things in the closet for Mercedes. "Is this the dress you're wearing for the company cookout tonight? It's gorgeous. And hey, this is the same blue as your pedicure! Confident women wear bold colors, you know, even on their toes."

Laughing, Mercedes pulled a nail polish bottle from the cosmetic purse she was unpacking for the bathroom. "I brought it in case I needed a touch-up for any chips I might get on the beach. Want to try it?"

Jana rushed to take the bottle out of Mercedes' hand, noting the brand and color name. "*Oceane.* Wow, I wish I hadn't already done mine."

"Yours is bold and beautiful, as well. I love that magenta! It's perfect for your coloring."

"Thanks! It goes well with what I'm wearing tonight, too. Feel like a walk on the beach?" Jana asked hopefully.

In minutes, they had on their swimsuits and carried totes with beach towels and paperbacks. Mercedes stopped in the kitchen for a small bag of frozen red grapes to put in a lunch sized cooler while Jana got bottles of cold water. Mercedes looked around for whomever might have watched them through the window earlier, but the house was quiet and empty.

The path to the beach stretched from the back door and deck to a long, weathered boardwalk spanning dune barriers with scraggly patches of tall grass. At the end, they settled their beach gear and flip-flops in the angled shade of shadows from the wooden steps, then they sank their feet into warm sand to reach the surf.

"If you don't care which direction we go, let's take this way," Jana suggested. "There's been a group of friendly dolphins swimming close to shore, even getting near people, and they mostly appear on this side. I'd love to see them!"

"I read about that in the little Bluffton community paper yesterday!" Mercedes exclaimed. "Oh, I do hope they show up."

They walked about fifteen minutes south, squinting against the brilliant sun on the sea and dodging ecstatic ball-chasing dogs, frisbees, horseshoes, and body boards. A smorgasbord of music styles rose as they passed cellphones and speakers blaring the favorite music of country, pop, hip-hop, and classic rock music fans. Mercedes relished a deep breath of salt breeze and satisfaction.

Then they saw a crowd gathering, looking out to the Atlantic and holding up cellphones. Mercedes and Jana scanned the contrast of sea and sky blues on the horizon, then their eyes roamed closer to shore. Dorsal fins that cusped like crescent moons bobbed in the waves, playing hide and seek with strong swimmers.

Elated, Mercedes and Jana reached for their cellphone cameras and aimed at the sight. Nearby, a knot of senior citizens discussed how two of the smaller young dolphins had finally nosed the marine biologist in the water and a couple of swimmers near him. "Their strongest sense of touch is in their noses and faces, you know," one of them said. "I heard they like to touch and are quite social." Another person in the group said, "Hey, did you hear what the top two most popular names for the pair are today? 'Freedom' and 'Liberty'!"

Mesmerized, Mercedes recorded several short videos, then changed the setting to Sports mode to photograph quick motion shots. Beside her, Jana gazed at her own phone video and breathed, "Oh, how beautiful! I'm going to text this to my sister and my parents."

Mercedes liked to evaluate her photos in the shade, without the glare of the sun over her screen, but she nodded. "They will love it! I'll wait until we get back to the house and pick the best ones to send. I also like to sketch and paint, and these may become reference photos."

"No kidding! How do you ever make time to paint?"

"It's a challenge, and I only finish a few a year. But it's a great way to relax."

"That's what I've heard. I hope you'll show me your work soon. Aw, looks like the dolphins are moving along. Sea birds are diving farther out in the ocean now—there must be a school of fish going by, and the dolphins want a snack," Jana pouted.

Beach goers reluctantly made way to their sand chairs, sandcastles, bright umbrellas, and beach towels. Jana and Mercedes turned back, strolling toward the house, keeping their toes in the spray and sea foam. Receding surf snagged on scattered seashells, abandoned by the last tide, creating ribbons of water that were erased by the edges of the next gentle wave.

The two friends strolled leisurely until they reached the location of the beach house boardwalk. Then they turned to the dunes toward their bags, ready to plop down in the sand

and relax. But when Jana grabbed her arm, Mercedes looked up and followed her friend's gaze.

Under a large canopy tent, a group gathered like a party was beginning. Hands reached into an open cooler and laughter rang out at jokes being shared. Upbeat music flowed, but it was subdued. And in the background corner shaded by the awning, a brunette stood too close to Zach. Her back was to Mercedes, but her right hand was in sight as she ran her fingertips playfully over his bare chest. Then she set her hand on her hip over the string of a yellow bikini and talked to him.

Declan noticed Mercedes and Jana and waved, trotting out to meet them. He pushed his sunglasses up on his head and grinned, then reached for Jana's hand. "We finished early today. I couldn't wait to get out to the beach and claim the most beautiful lady on it!"

He greeted Mercedes and asked how they had spent the day. Jana launched into a brief itinerary of lunch and the dolphin encounter, while Mercedes nodded in support now and then and smiled absently. She was over the initial shock and stab of pain at seeing Zach let another woman touch him intimately, in front of all his future co-workers. She focused on Declan and Jana.

Zach called out, and they turned, watching him jog toward them with his usual athletic grace. When he reached Mercedes' side, he pecked a lightning-fast kiss on her cheek. Then he draped his arm around her shoulders, relaxed and smiling, as if she hadn't stiffened under his touch.

"We finished early," he announced. "I saw your Jeep in the drive and looked for you, but they said you were at the beach."

Mercedes and Jana locked eyes. Jana said, "We didn't see anyone in the house, and told no one we were coming to the beach. Who mentioned that?"

Zach shrugged and looked at Declan. Dark sunglasses hid his eyes, so Mercedes couldn't read them when he said, "I don't know, really. Maybe Declan remembers."

Declan's tone was testy. "I wasn't with you. I assumed they were at the beach because I knocked on their door and they weren't in their room."

"What difference does it make?" asked Zach with another nonchalant shrug. He grinned at Mercedes and pulled her a little closer. "The important thing is that you're here with me. Come on, you need to meet some people with the firm."

Declan kept his hold on Jana's hand, and like Mercedes, they silently followed Zach to the shade of the tent. Other women had come out to join the group now, and they introduced themselves as attorneys or as wives of some of the other attorneys. The young woman who was too friendly with Zach came to introduce herself as Jill, Mr. Lenoir's secretary.

Mercedes' mind seized on something. She had paid scant attention when Zach mentioned the name of the law group he hoped to work for. Now she recalled it and noted that Lenoir Bassett was not a man's name. It was two last names! An uneasy feeling washed over her.

"It's good to meet you at last, Mercedes. We've kept Zach so busy that he hasn't told us anything about you," said Jill in a honeyed voice.

"Oh, then he's in his element! Zach thrives on staying busy," replied Mercedes with a pleasant smile, keeping her tone silvery. "The past year, he lived and breathed his law school degree, and now he's living for this opportunity to join the firm. We've met a few times to go out together, but there's not much he could tell you about me. I'm only here because I rented a fabulous cottage nearby for the summer, working with clients in Bluffton."

Zach froze on his way to her with a bottle of flavored sparkling water from the cooler. His eyes were unreadable behind sunglasses, but Jill's had a passing look of alarm.

A happy melody rose from the phone in the pocket of Mercedes' sheer mesh cover-up, contrasting with the classic rock song on the stereo under the canopy. She shrugged and smiled apologetically. "Will you please excuse me, Jill? I'm waiting on an important call, and this could be it." She drew the phone out, turning to the boardwalk to move away from the music and clamor of voices at the party.

Chapter 5

"Hi, Mom!" said Mercedes into her phone, with more enthusiasm than she felt. Her mother would sense her mood, and this was no place to get into a discussion about it. After a brief greeting, her mom reported she had an update about the document photos Mercedes had sent. The paper trail supporting the deed in the cedar chest originated with a family named Lenoir. The property had changed owners twice, then it was signed over to the Ellisons. Roland Lenoir was the one who sold it. Every Lenoir descendant since that time attempted to get the land back, but these were legally futile, and Mercedes' father had not been aware of one in his lifetime. Four direct descendants of the original Lenoir family were still living, and one was an attorney named Stanley Lenoir. He had a son and two married daughters.

Mercedes gently bit her lip and her gaze roamed over the scraggly dune grass and blooming daisy-like yellow flowers on the ground cover at the back of the beach house. "Mom, did the research have a record of where Stanley Lenoir works as an attorney?"

"Oh, let's see," her mother's voice trailed. Mercedes knew the keys were flying on her laptop computer. "Here it is. Yes, he's been quite successful. He's a partner with Lenoir Bassett and Madigan, P.C. It's a boutique law firm, based out of Atlanta. They have several offices around the Southeast."

It was surreal—and true. But did her mother need to know about Zach's goal of working with the firm, and that Mercedes was visiting among the employees right now? Did she need to know that her daughter would meet Mr. Stanley Lenoir tonight or tomorrow?

Mercedes struggled, trying to imagine what she would expect of her own daughter. This was no confidential matter, and it may have far-reaching implications for her family.

"Mercedes?"

"Mom, there's something I have to tell you," Mercedes said, glancing back at the party tent to judge the distance. Her bare feet sank ankle-deep into warm sand as she took a few more steps away. As simply as she could, she explained her situation. "As soon as I settle something with Zach and help a new Christian friend, I'll return to Bluffton," she said. "I told her I'd support her to talk to her boyfriend about some New Age training he and Zach had here. I'm with many people and not likely to be in any danger."

Danger? Why had that come out of her mouth?

Her mother was quiet for a few moments, then said, "I understand you didn't know all this when you went to the island to meet Zach. But you know now. This is not a coincidence, sweetheart. Pray for discernment and listen to your intuition. Please call me tonight to update me about what's happening and where you are."

Mercedes ended the call with her mother and pressed her fingers to her lips. The cheerful beach setting, the brilliant sunlight, made it difficult to grasp the dark truth about the gravity and absurdity of her situation. In her gut, she knew that something was happening behind the scenes, invisible to her. She could never explain times like these.

Then she looked up to see someone watching her from behind a nearby dune that led to a public beach access. The dune hid most of his body and he was as unrecognizable as any tall guy on the beach in a baseball cap, dark sunglasses, a beach towel around his neck, and a sloppy wet tee shirt over swim shorts. Instantly, he looked down and disappeared up the path.

Mercedes jumped and dragged her eyes from where the stranger vanished when Zach's arms encircled her from behind. Her flimsy coverup was open in front, and he clasped his hands over the silky waist of her swimsuit. In her ear, he whispered, "You're the most beautiful woman on the beach."

His breath tickled on her neck, sending a shiver over her shoulder. She slid her phone toward her coverup pocket and turned. He adjusted his arms to rest on the small of her back and stood looking down into her face with an intensity of attraction that sent a thrill through her. Declan and Jana came up to join them.

"You and Declan traded notes. Jana's supposed to be the most beautiful," she said, smiling.

"Ah, and I hear you and Jana traded notes, too," he shot back, keeping her circled in one arm as they turned to laugh with Declan. His chest was no longer bare for Jill's touch. He wore a tee shirt bearing the emblem of his favorite designer over his heart.

Jana smiled and turned a knowing look at Mercedes. "I told them we want to talk to them when we can all get together."

"Sooner rather than later, I'm afraid," Mercedes responded, keeping her voice light. "Something came up and I need to get back to the cottage."

Coolly, she pulled her sunglasses down from her head to cover her eyes. Declan mildly protested her proposal about leaving, Jana became alert, and Zach's brows knit together in a scowl. "It's rude to leave the group on the beach right now, and then there's the cookout tonight," he said. "We can get away afterwards, maybe come down here on the beach, but you shouldn't be leaving here in the dark, babe. Stay tonight, and we'll see what tomorrow brings. Is there anything I can do?"

Mercedes paused. "You're right, it would be rude to leave now, and I don't want to spoil your celebration cookout. It's a family matter I need to focus on."

Jana asked, "Is everything okay? Anyone hurt?"

Mercedes knew better than to lie, but she must be evasive. "Oh—it's nothing like that. You see, I discovered some family records in an antique cedar hope chest I picked up at an estate auction. My parents are doing research about the documents, and with my background in historic records, I could be a lot of help."

"Wow, that's fascinating!" exclaimed Jana.

"Oh, I get it. Any interesting skeletons in the closet?" quipped Declan, winking at Zach.

When she hesitated again, Declan's grin disappeared. Zach turned her face to his with a finger. "Mercedes?"

In a flash, she understood his concern was not for her feelings. It was for anything that might be a negative for his future if they should be together. Lenoir Bassett and Madigan wanted her in his life.

She managed a blithe smile and a slight wave of her hand. "Oh, mercy, no, my family is too perfect for me to live up to, in fact. But there was once a legal conflict over land before we came to America, and we will clear it up once and for all. So, you can see how my expertise in property evaluation is helpful."

Declan chuckled and said, "Wow, Zach, this sounds a bit like the hypothetical case in the firm's contest last year in law school." He turned to Jana. "Zach won. In his scenario, marriage could legally take the land between—"

Zach dropped his arm and drew back as if Mercedes burned him. But Jill was right there in his place, taking Mercedes' arm and pulling her to the canopy. "Come on, you guys, join the party!"

Reeling from Declan's revelation, Mercedes let her arm go taunt before she obeyed. Jana called, "I'll get our things from the stairs."

Munching frozen grapes and sipping sparkling water, Mercedes and Jana hung around the outer edges of the party under the canopy. Jana murmured that conversation with people who were drinking was pointless. Within minutes, crude jokes trumpeted by loose tongues made Mercedes and Jana cringe. Shedding their cover-ups and sunglasses, they walked to the edge of the water to swim, squinting against the sun's glare on the Atlantic Ocean. "Mercedes, what happened? Why did your family history startle Zach? Is it really like the hypothetical scenario in his brief?"

"I don't know. If he mentioned his assignment to me last year, I don't recall it. Does Declan have any idea about why we want to talk to them?"

"He must suspect it, from my reaction the first day. He never mentions his 'number' to me anymore, but I hear others talking about theirs. Did you hear the ladies under the tent describing how they tailored their shopping choices this morning to their 'number'?"

Mercedes sighed. "Yes, I did, among other conversation that I wish I hadn't heard. And believe me, Jana, if I was ready, I would share with you about the family thing and how it affects Zach. But I only found out an hour ago, and I need time to mull it all over. I can say that my parents are uneasy about me staying here tonight, and I must leave tomorrow. You've probably already sensed that my relationship with Zach has unofficially ended. It never really had a chance."

"Are you upset?"

"No. I might have wavered if I hadn't seen him allow Jill's touch, but now I know he's already wandered away. He needs his freedom."

They swam near each other, letting the waves pound their bodies for a natural massage. Mercedes finally told Jana she was ready to go get their things to dry off and then rest before dressing for the cookout. As they walked together toward the canopy, Jana asked, "Mercedes, are you in any danger?"

"I honestly don't know."

The group of attorneys welcomed them back to the shade of the canopy with a few whistles of admiration, a sure sign that the cooler was nearly empty. When Mercedes and Jana said they were going inside and would be down on the deck in time for the company cookout, Declan said he was ready to go back, too, and would escort them.

Zach fleetingly touched Mercedes' hand. "Looking forward to seeing you tonight."

"Me, too," she said. "We really need to talk, Zach. Alone."

He nodded soberly. "I know. I'll manage it somehow."

She smiled, then turned to the boardwalk to follow Jana and Declan.

Mercedes set her beach tote bag down on the sprawling deck of the vacation house. "Hey, you two lovebirds, go on in. I want to have a look around."

Jana stood straight and alert, squeezing Declan's hand. He glanced at her with a question in his eyes as she said, "If you think you're getting out of my sight, think again. Declan, I'll text you in a while."

Declan shook his head and his finger at them. "Ah, ah, ah! No way I'm letting you two spooky women go without seeing what you're up to. Which way?"

Mercedes stared at him as if mulling something over, lips pursed. Then she shrugged. "Okay. I want to see what's on the side of the house opposite the other beach house."

"No problem," he quipped, ushering them down the deck stairs and into the sandy back yard. "I'm game for exploring. I've seen traffic there and a small sign about parking. It may be a beach access. Could be busy on weekends."

Declan was right. Through a grove of scruffy pines and a variety of palms, there was a low wall, about two feet high and covered in rough tabby. On the other side, scattered vehicles parked in a sandy lot. The fortunate ones found shelter in the shade of overhanging trees along the edges of the property.

"What next?" asked Declan with a roguish grin. "Do we jump it? I forgot my Indiana Jones hat."

"No. Like you, I'm not dressed for extreme sports," Mercedes quipped, glancing down at her modest bathing suit under the mesh cover-up. She shaded her eyes with her hand from the blinding glare of a windshield. "Over there, past the pickup truck, could the path lead to a narrow boardwalk down to the beach? I thought I saw one this afternoon." *And a spy on it.*

This time, Jana piped up. "Yeah, there is. I got confused one day and walked up to it, instead of the one at the back of the house. Did you see something suspicious over there?"

Before Mercedes could answer, she flinched and gasped. Her friends followed her gaze and saw nothing unusual. "What?" asked Declan.

Then they followed her over the wall, landing in front of a sign posted on it, warning against trespassing. She briskly slapped her hands together to brush away hard bits of tabby, then threaded her way through the parked vehicles until she stopped beside a white sedan parked in the shade. But there was no shadowy form behind the tinted window to show a driver was inside.

Unnerved, Declan exclaimed, "What gives, Mercedes? I thought I might have to fight somebody who didn't appreciate you showing up at his door!"

Jana slapped her hand to her chest and let out a long breath. "Mercedes, you scared me."

Mercedes peered inside to see a cooler on the seat and a briefcase on the front floorboard. In the back seat, there was a folded beach towel. The vehicle was neat and clean. Obviously flustered, she walked around it and studied the tag. "I think this car has been following me, and I caught a man watching me on the beach today at the public access," she said. "I was ending a call with my mom and looked up. He looked down, as if nothing happened. He doesn't mean any harm to me. But I can't shake the feeling that something is off."

"Is he handsome?" Jana ventured.

Declan scowled. "I see a thousand cars just like this on the road every day. Nothing special," he said. "Tags are from this state. Why would anyone follow you?"

"I hoped I could meet the guy and ask," Mercedes said levelly. "And yes, Jana, he's tall, dark, and handsome. Ruggedly so, the outdoorsy type."

"Let's go down to the beach again and look for him," suggested Jana. Declan playfully slapped at her.

Mercedes shook her head. "No, Zach and the others would notice us. Things could get awkward." She took out her cell phone and photographed the sedan from different angles. Then she gasped.

"What now?" breathed Jana, coming to her shoulder. "Being with you is like riding a roller coaster!"

"It looks like someone has handled my phone."

"How can you tell?" Jana asked. "Show me. Don't you have a password or something?"

Holding the device in her hand, Mercedes looked off into the distance, trying to remember. "After I finished the call with my mom, I got distracted for a second with the guy watching me, then Zach came up behind me," she began slowly. "He was all arms, and I thought I dropped my phone in my pocket. It may still have been open to my home screen. Maybe it just got touched accidentally several times and made some changes."

"I followed you, watching Jill pull you like she was on a mission," said Jana.

Declan narrowed his eyes as he said, "I started following, but I turned to say something to Zach about that case we mentioned, expecting him to be right behind me. But he was still where we left him, looking at what I assumed was his phone. He cupped it in his hand, so I didn't notice, and said he'd catch up in a few minutes."

Mercedes and Jana searched his eyes, and he spread his hands in surrender. "Jana, you know I wouldn't make something like that up! Maybe Mercedes dropped her phone, and he picked it up off the sand. That's a good thing, right? Or maybe he just got a notification on his own phone."

Jana looked at Mercedes. "Show us what looks different."

Mercedes pointed to her screen. "I use an encrypted text service, and when I text someone, their name goes to the top," she explained. "The last text I sent today was you, Jana. But your name is third—after Zach and my mom. I didn't text my mom today, but someone could have looked at hers and interacted with it—like copy and paste, or forwarding, or something like that. I'm also careful about deleting texts I read that are no longer relevant, mainly just to keep away clutter, but also to protect confidential information for clients and friends."

"Open the line for Zach," Declan said.

She clicked on Zach's name, and the last text was two days ago. "The one I sent last night isn't here. There wasn't anything much in it, just that I had made plans with Jana and would arrive today for lunch. I said I'd pack for the weekend and looked forward to seeing him."

"Did he text back last night?" Jana asked. "Declan said he sat with Jill at dinner and came back with her group."

"I was in bed when he got back, maybe an hour later. And he was in a rush this morning," said Declan.

Mercedes sighed. "No, he didn't text me back at all. But if he was forwarding or copying something from my other texts and didn't want me to know, he would have deleted them out. He could have accidentally deleted the text from last night."

She closed the line for Zach and opened her mother's communications. "Mom's texts are here, and I wouldn't know if he interacted with them. But..." her voice trailed off in thought.

"But what?" Jana's tone was impatient.

"Most of the messages were about the family issues, the documents I mentioned on the beach. I snapped photos of some journal pages with names on them for her to research. If Zach did in fact rescue my phone and he checked who I've been in contact with, he may have seen those photos."

Jana rubbed her face in her hands. "You should bring this up with Zach, just in case. Like you pointed out, it could be nothing more than the screen going crazy after you put it in your pocket, right? Either that's what happened, or Zach rescued it and put it back there when you left your coverup to go swimming."

Mercedes slowly nodded, still puzzling. Declan twisted around, scrutinizing the parking area. There was no one he could see spying on them. But he noticed where the wall ended, and he led the ladies back to the house. "And I thought I was teasing when I described you as spooky," he muttered.

Swimming and sleuthing left Jana and Mercedes ravenous, and Declan followed them into the beach house kitchen to make a snack. There seemed to be no one around. Mercedes learned that while this house was upscale, the interior of the firm's next beach house was opulent. Lenoir, Bassett, and Madigan used that lodging when they spent time on the island.

"What do you know about the partners?" Mercedes asked before she bit a slice of apple.

Declan finished chewing a cracker laden with deli meat, cheese, and an olive. "Nothing much about their personal lives. They aren't among the families that run the world and don't run in the circles of the families that run the world, but they lurk somewhere in the fringes of the circles of the circles who run the world."

"If you learned the firm was doing anything illegal, or had questionable practices, what would you do?" asked Mercedes.

"Well—honestly, I haven't thought about that angle. I imagine there are safeguards that protect the attorneys who aren't criminals. My actions would depend on the situation. I would need to make sure there was no link to myself."

Jana wiped up the kitchen island, then she and Mercedes put the snack items back in the refrigerator. She suggested they give Mercedes a quick tour of the house in case they got separated, and when they ended the tour in their own room, they took a nap before time to dress for dinner.

Chapter 6

Jana swung the door wide when a brisk knock assaulted it, and her boyfriend whistled in admiration. "New dress?" he asked.

She nodded, and Mercedes came up behind her, pulling on a shoe and straightening a small purse across her body. Her eyes met his after scanning for Zach to be there, and he announced brightly, "I have the honor of escorting you both down to dinner. Zach got called to a meeting about half an hour ago. The place is buzzing with royalty—namely, Lenoir, Bassett, and Madigan, who will occupy the palace next to these humble slave quarters."

Tilting her head and setting her hands on her hips, Jana demanded, "Why weren't you called to the same meeting?"

Declan shrugged, making a sweep of his arm to point them down the hall. "I'm not on Jill's VIP list."

Jana leaned over to plant a kiss on his cheek. "But you're on mine."

He wiggled his brows up and down at her and winked at Mercedes. "That's the one that counts, Princess. Does the house still feel strange to you?"

"It's not as oppressive since Mercedes arrived. She brought sunbeams," Jana replied, turning a smile to her friend.

They checked in with the kitchen staff to determine what it would serve and when Jana and Mercedes should come for what they may need for their special diets. They learned there were other guests with dietary limitations, and the menu was kept simple as a farm-to-table affair to accommodate the most people possible.

Since they had their favorite flavored sparkling water in the refrigerator, Jana and Mercedes poured it into glasses set out for guests. They exchanged pleasantries with some wives and attorneys as they made their way out to the deck, where the sea breeze was a cool caress, and the sky promised romantic twilight.

Mercedes seemed to be the only unescorted woman in the group, and though Jana and Declan were wonderful at including her, a pang of loneliness stabbed her heart. Behind a pasted-on smile, she prayed again for the strength, wisdom, and grace she needed to endure the evening. Manners demanded that she remain until they served the food.

Wandering away from her friends to find a measure of peace in an expansive view of the sea, Mercedes went to the deck railing. Tranquility was the payoff for a few minutes, but then Zach and Jill appeared on the boardwalk. Slanted sun rays spotlighted his blazer and dress khakis. The breeze stirred his tawny brown hair, giving him the air of a rogue, and she supposed he was one. Was Jill on her way to being her replacement?

Longing for something real, a true love in her life, she was on the brink of turning away when she realized the pair was in a heated discussion. With a look of disgust, he stormed away from Jill and looked up at the crowd gathering on the deck.

Mercedes waited at the deck railing for Zach to notice her and realize she saw him with Jill—again. When he spotted her watching, he waved and started jogging her way. At the bottom step, he looked up to grin sheepishly and motioned to her to wait while he shook sand from his shoes. Then he hopped up the stairs and had eyes only for her.

"Oh, Mercedes, you don't know how good it is to see you," he said breathlessly, pulling her possessively into a hug and planting a kiss on the top of her hair. "You're stunning! That dress is the color of the ocean and your hair shimmers like sand." He ran his fingers lightly down a length of silky blonde hair and his eyes softened. With a glance around, he murmured, "I wish we could get away from here."

She smiled at him and settled his bangs. "And every time we're together, I'm with the best-looking guy around. Your afternoon on the beach really paid off with that tan. We'll get away, after dinner. Why were you on the boardwalk just now?"

"I got a text about a work-related meeting, something Jill needed to tell me before I meet the owners of the firm. They are here and will be down later. She said the only privacy was on the boardwalk. That may be true but meeting alone can lead to misunderstandings."

Declan and Jana came over, bringing an extra sparkling water with a lemon slice for Zach. Jill had ascended the stairs and was mixing with another group near an outdoor kitchen, where mouth-watering aromas rose from the grills.

Zach murmured his gratitude for the drink and had several sips. "Does anyone know how long it will be until dinner?"

"Not much longer, or it will be overcooked," observed Jana. "Is everything okay, Zach?"

Zach nodded, then took another sip from his glass. "Yeah, no worries. But let's disappear after we eat."

"Oh, here are the guests of honor," Declan noted, pointing his glass to a row of French doors. Several men with women on their arms were slowly moving out onto the deck, and mild applause rose from the other attorneys to honor their employers, Lenoir, Bassett, and Madigan. It was a casual entrance, with the three partners shaking hands with established employees and being introduced to the new recruits.

"Which one is which?" Jana asked in a low voice.

"The one with salt and pepper hair is Lenoir, a picture of craft and composure." It was out of her mouth before she thought twice, and Zach and Declan turned to look at her with brows raised. She closed her eyes and sipped from her glass.

Jana kept her eyes on the man and said solemnly, "Yes, he has the classic look of belonging in a semi-legitimate world where currency is bargains, tricks, lies, and betrayals."

Astonished, Declan whispered, "Did you two look him up online or something? This isn't a novel; it's a company cookout."

Mercedes shrugged lightly and replied, "No, I didn't. I can't explain it, I just knew."

Zach studied her while Declan said, "I mean it, you ladies are the spookiest people I've ever met. Zach, you should have been on our adventure this afternoon. Mercedes has evidence that she's under surveillance."

A passing look of alarm fled from Zach's face when Stanley Lenoir was suddenly before them, introducing himself and his wife in a confident, gravelly voice. Mrs. Lenoir's heavily accented English suited her sultry manner. She was gracious, ready to move on to the next group of people. But since her arm remained tucked into Mr. Lenoir's, she smiled and settled beside him.

Zach and Declan introduced themselves and their dates. Mercedes barely let her eyes glance into Lenoir's face as she half-smiled and nodded. Declan answered a question from Lenoir about the sessions they attended to learn more about the firm, and Mercedes smiled absently, looking over at the next couple, where Bassett and Madigan were making small talk, waiting on their turn to meet Zach and Declan.

"Miss Ellison, I hear you know quite a lot about antiquities. I dabble at collecting pieces now and then. We have something in common."

Startled that he addressed her directly, Mercedes looked up and nodded as she replied, "Oh—yes, I've worked in archaeological excavation sites and traveled with my parents over the years. I've visited many history museums, but I'm certain you're far more knowledgeable than I am. My family's collection isn't extensive. In fact, the oldest thing we've gained recently is an antique cedar chest, the kind young ladies once called a 'hope chest.' It was a remarkable find, an unlisted item at an estate auction I came upon. Then a carpenter who is restoring it discovered a hidden compartment with important old family deeds and documents stored there. It's the kind of thing that inspires romantic theories."

She turned a winsome smile up at Zach, who had paled, then she met Lenoir's smoldering eyes. A spark of understanding passed between them before Mr. Bassett came to stand beside Lenoir, joking about wanting to meet the new recruits so they could all have dinner while it was hot.

"My word, what happened?" gasped Jana after Bassett and Madigan moved Lenoir along to eat. "Did you see his eyes when he met yours? They were positively predatory!"

Jana and Mercedes gathered with their dates at a buffet table laden with scrumptious seafood, filet mignon, and roasted chicken. Kabobs speared vegetables and fruit bearing perfectly charred stripes from the grill, and Mercedes inhaled the mix of delicious aromas before she murmured, "I honestly didn't plan to say anything about my family's discovery, but it was out before I could stop. He intentionally opened a door that revealed who he is and that he's aware of who I am. Now I know what I'm dealing with."

Zach nervously selected food for his plate and leaned in to ask if he could put some on for Mercedes. She nodded and thrust her plate closer to him, grateful that he was detail oriented enough to learn what she could eat. He reached with his long arm to get something, especially for her. She beamed up at him appreciatively, and he leaned in to plant a fleeting kiss on her feathery bangs.

When they found a table where all four could sit together, Declan offered to say a blessing over the meal. It was quiet and quick, for their ears only, but they opened their eyes to see several curious onlookers. Zach was nonchalant as he cut his steak into smaller bites, but his voice was tight when he said, "Mercedes, don't leave my side for any reason. Is that clear?"

She looked up sharply, then back down. She said, "I think we are all on the same page, sticking together tonight."

"No, we aren't all on the same page," Zach said testily. "You shared something important with Declan and Jana that you haven't told me."

"And I wonder if you have something important you haven't shared with me, too," she retorted, keeping her voice low.

Zach glanced up at her, then around their table, swallowing his bite of food and taking a sip of tea before he responded by saying, "I want Declan and Jana to know this because you're sharing a room tonight with her. Recently, I opened my mail back in Virginia and had a typed note warning me not to involve Mercedes in—"

He paused, then said, "In my business with the firm. I'm not yet willing to disclose more than that. The note claimed to be from a friend."

Declan stopped chewing and stared at Zach, wide-eyed. Jana asked if he had any idea who the friend might be, but Zach shook his head and replied, "I wavered between thinking the note was a joke by friends who knew how much I want this job, or some set-up test by the firm that would play out during the training the past few days. Now, I'm rattled. I learned something last night that made me question everything. I've been selfish and stupid, and I need help to sort out what to do next. Let's finish dinner and find a private place to talk."

On the dark side of twilight, Zach rolled up the hems of his khakis and waited for Mercedes to put her shoes on the beach house boardwalk. He firmly tugged at her hand, helping her through soft mounds of sand, while Declan and Jana tagged behind them. A halo formed around a beclouded moon and stars were revealing their whereabouts.

"Oh," breathed Mercedes. "I never get enough of evening skies over the ocean."

Zach moved close behind her, circling his arms around her waist. He whispered huskily, "Yes, it's perfect, if only—if things were different."

They basked in the panoramic view and curling waves before them. Lacy surf frills sparkled and teased their toes and tiny glittering lights from fishing boats and dinner cruises hovered near the horizon.

"What's that?" asked Jana, pointing up the beach to the north.

Reluctant to break the spell of their own private moment, Zach and Mercedes stayed where they were, only turning their heads toward Jana's mystery. A black silhouetted pier stretched out into the water.

Declan answered, "That's the boat dock. There's private access down there for the owners of the properties on this street, and some guys are taking a boat out fishing tomorrow morning. The firm owns one."

At the mention of the firm, Zach's arms fell from around Mercedes. "Declan, let's walk a little farther down the beach for some privacy and spread out that blanket you brought."

The friends found a good place to sit together. Zach sat cross-legged with his hands clasped, then cleared his throat. "Confession time. Mercedes," he began. "I found your phone on the sand today after Jill pulled you to the canopy. I was going to close the screen and bring it to you, but it was open to your photos. Seeing documents instead of views of the cottage or something like that, I was wildly curious. You had just mentioned a family issue over research, and I learned things at dinner last night that made me suspicious. I opened a couple of them and confirmed what I didn't want to know. I put it back in your cover-up while you were away swimming."

Mercedes nodded slowly. "Did you look at my texts?"

"Not exactly. I sent a few of the documents to myself. I don't know why I was sneaky about it since I planned to tell you, anyway. But I deleted them afterwards. Honestly, I believe if I'd just asked you, you would have shared them with me. I didn't scroll through to see if you're texting any other guys, but near the top was your mom's name, and it showed you'd sent a photo. I clicked it to make sure I was on the right track with the document but read nothing and didn't scroll through."

He reached for her hand and peered into her face. "I am so incredibly sorry, Mercedes," he said. "I hope this won't change the trust level between us. I'm a jerk in more ways than you know. What I did was inexcusable, but if you'll consider an excuse anyway, I'm off-kilter these days and nothing is what it seems. My future is at stake and it's time I got my mind wrapped around facts about the situation I'm in. I've dragged you into something and need to get you out of it. Please, will you forgive me?"

She nodded slowly. "Yes, you're forgiven, but as you said, if you could have waited and asked, I would have shown you."

"She knew someone had handled her phone, in the parking lot, when she took photos of the white car," Jana put in.

He held out his hand. "A white car? May I see the photos?"

Mercedes pulled her small cross-body bag around to open it. She found the gallery and set it to the first pictures, then handed it to him.

Declan chuckled. "You should've seen her, Zach. She marched to the driver's side like she was law enforcement or something, and I just knew I'd have to fight some guy who didn't appreciate having her in his personal space. But the car was empty. The only things inside were a cooler, a flight-bag type of leather briefcase, and a beach towel folded in the back seat."

"I saw the car twice in Bluffton, and a man watching me at the public access earlier today. I didn't tell you sooner because I wondered if I was imagining things. You're all about logic and evidence, not my intuition."

Zach studied the photos of the white car, then met Mercedes' eyes. "I believe you, and you can't go back to Bluffton tonight, not after all this. Stay here." He swept his arm toward Declan and Jana. "Let's try to solve this, together."

Jana grabbed Mercedes' arm. "He's right, you know. You don't believe the spy in the car will harm you, but he reports to someone. He parked right beside the house—what if that someone is here? You may be in the lion's den, but at least you aren't alone."

Declan's eyes challenged Zach. "Zach, are you totally with us? I haven't told Jana or Mercedes what I saw last night, and you've been acting weird today, to put it mildly. We need a confession about Jill."

Groaning and raking his clawed fingers through his hair, Zach made a growling sound. He explained how he had gotten hooked up with the secretary before dinner and how he worked on the time spent with her to find out why Mr. Lenoir wanted to meet his girlfriend, and why it mattered that he and Mercedes got married. He added, "Jill said Mercedes was the reason I was being hired, and I said no, I had the firm's attention by winning the hypothetical case contest right before meeting her. It was then that my alarm bells went off. Were you ever pressured about Jana, Declan?"

"Not really," Declan said. "They just stressed that the company prefers their attorneys, both men and women, to be married. I don't know, maybe single people are more prone to end up in bars and share confidential information after a few drinks. It was a plus for me."

He squeezed Jana's hand and said, "I'm in a serious relationship and I seriously want it to get more serious."

"When I started thinking back, I realized meeting Mercedes at the conference could easily have been a plan. There were no guarantees we would hit it off, but look at her—how could I not try? And as a law student applying to firms, I knew I was being watched." Zach looked over at Mercedes with a weak grin. "This sounds like a stretch, but I'm ditching my logical thinking and evidence and switching to intuition on this. I've learned to trust my instincts more since meeting you."

"Zach, do you know what you're implying?" asked Jana.

"I do now, thanks to what Mercedes told us today about her family, then what I saw in the private photos of documents she has. I leave it up to her about how much she can say. There is more to the note I received in the mail. The writer claimed the firm is under investigation. He or she did not say what for, or why I should not get Mercedes involved. But how under heaven did the author of the note associate her with the firm and the investigation to begin with? Something doesn't add up. Or it does, and I haven't caught up yet."

Mercedes and Zach sat, looking solemnly at one another. She said, "The Lenoir family and mine go back for many years. The connection involves disputed property and murder. I never knew this until a few days ago, when the hidden compartment of the cedar chest revealed documents and a journal."

She sighed, then said, "But my parents and grandparents knew. Maybe my brother knows, as well. As for me, I can only guess why Mr. Lenoir wants to meet me and draw me into his company."

"I can tell you why, but maybe Zach would prefer to," growled Declan.

"The paper that gave me a shot with Lenoir Bassett and Madigan was about how to resolve such a land dispute," Zach said flatly. "The short version is, I stated that time had shown laws will not permit someone to force a sale of the land or prove any claim to it. I proposed a marriage scenario to gain the land in a couple's assets. Either through divorce or another means of selling the land, by consent or coercion, the person trying to get the land can use the situation to their advantage."

Mercedes gasped, and Jana's hand flew to her mouth. Declan was steady, with a hard look at Zach and deliberate words. "Assuming Lenoir is the same family as the one in the Ellisons' past, if you marry her, he could work a way to coerce or blackmail you to get the land back, or make sure it's in your part of a divorce settlement and buy it from you. Any scenario makes Jill a useful tool."

Zach's head drooped as he nodded to the blanket. He looked up and stared out at the softly rolling sea. "She's laying the groundwork," he replied. "Last night, she told me marriage to Mercedes was no obstacle, and before the cookout tonight, she asked me out to the boardwalk for what she said was business. I expected some other employees to be there, but it was only us. In a nutshell, she reminded me of how rare an opportunity it is to join the company, since I'm not a woman and I'm so unfortunate as to be a white male, both of which will limit my chances to get decent job offers or loans to open a firm on my own these days."

He made a short snorting sound and then said, "She's right. I already fought the discrimination battles through college, and they are real. It cost me a lot more money and time than necessary to get my degree because they kicked my higher scores out to admit lesser ones."

Declan sighed. "He's right, and Jill's right. I've been there. But she's using it as leverage to manipulate you, Zach. Has she made any physical advances? Don't be alone with her anymore. She can't accuse you of accosting her if you can prove you were somewhere else."

Zach nodded. "Yes, she has, but we weren't totally alone, and I was on guard and deflected her without being blunt. I would never have gone to the boardwalk if I suspected."

He turned to Mercedes. "You saw the end of that encounter, right? Did I look like a man having a rendezvous with a lover on the side?"

She shook her head. "No, you were angry. When I first saw you this afternoon, you let her touch your chest, but you didn't reach back for her or act as if you invited it. You pulled on a tee shirt afterwards."

He snorted bitterly and shook his head, then said, "That was your first impression of me, after not seeing each other in person for what, two months now?"

"We've never defined our relationship, Zach," Mercedes said. "I think Declan and Jana know we're in a transition grounded in whether you get this job, and for all I knew, Jill was part of the process. I enjoy spending time with you when we meet up and go out, but most of our relationship is spent on phone calls and texting. We can never know one another that way. I was going to end as friends this weekend, with an open door when you're ready to focus on a woman in your life, but now, I'm not sure whether that will help or hurt your chances with Lenoir, Bassett, and Madigan."

Zach's expression closed. After an awkward stretch filled by the relentless ebb and flow of the surf, Jana said, "Maybe it would be better to keep up the appearance of a serious relationship. It may keep Mercedes safe."

Chapter 8

Dangling his flip-flops in his fingers and sitting on a sandy boardwalk step, the antiquities investigator held a cellphone to his ear. "It's not a beach party, I can say that. I tagged along behind another group who were strolling under the stars, and the little foursome on the beach blanket is tense. I'd be losing myself in conjecture to report anything more."

"You're confirming what I've been told. The partners have arrived at the business event. A fly on the wall sent me a photo of Mercedes and Lenoir in an exchange of words when he asked her about antiquities. Wow, that's some dress, hey?"

The young man blew out a breath. He would never admit how distracting that dress was. "Antiquities?" he squeaked, throwing off his baseball cap to the sand at the bottom of a dune and running his hand through his hair. "He didn't even have dinner before he started dragging her into his web. Does she sense anything is wrong?"

"Not to worry—yet. Zach seems to have caught on, and one photo that I have leaves no doubt she and Lenoir know they will never be friends. She held her own and upped his game."

"Upped his game? What does that mean?"

"It means he didn't know her family recently came into possession of some important documents, and he's not sure if she just super-sized his happy meal or ran over it."

The young man shot to his feet and stabbed the night air with his finger. "You send me that photo and you keep her safe.

A few kids can't outsmart a man with no fear of God or dread of the devil."

Mercedes and her friends sat stretched on a blanket, enjoying one another's companionship. Zach had shaken off any rejection from her revelation about their relationship status and stuck close by.

Declan ventured, "Hey, Jana, you said you had something to talk about. Is it still on your mind?"

"Yes," she replied. "I haven't heard you and Zach talking about your personality 'numbers' since your first day of training sessions, but other employees are."

"Oh, well, that's based on the books I showed you," Declan said. "Jill led a session in our training so we can know our true selves better, but it was mumbo-jumbo to me. I haven't had time to read the books."

Jana turned to face him. "As a Christian, can you tell me how self-focus squares with scripture?"

Declan looked at her blankly. "Scripture?"

Jana rolled her eyes and said, "You know, the measure and standard for Christians to study and follow, once they choose heaven's perspective on life and turn from the world's ways?"

He bumped his shoulder against hers and grinned. "I know what the Bible is," he replied. "I just don't get the connection."

"The connection is, we evaluate philosophies in life from a biblical standpoint," Jana answered. "Scripture never teaches there is a 'true self' or that we should seek enlightenment, wisdom, and answers within ourselves. But it tells us *not* to, and Ecclesiastes is full of warnings against seeking fulfillment that way. Our purpose is to seek God and change to be like Him. We become new creations with redemption through Christ's blood, as in John 14:6. When that happens, there is no taking a 'road back to you' because Jesus set you free from that road and expects you to walk with Him on another one. Everything is about Jesus—all the answers, all the glory."

"Oh. I didn't realize..." Declan trailed off. "I mean, of course, I believe everything you said. It's obvious, really. I simply didn't apply that to the training topic. I probably would have seen that once I read the books."

"It's just a tool," Zach commented, shrugging. "There doesn't have to be anything religious about it."

Mercedes remembered what her Bible Study leader advised her about presenting information to Zach. She said, "One author and proponent of the teachings claims they are often misunderstood as simply a personality tool to identify and describe traits. He doesn't agree and he teaches a works-based theology behind them. Do you have standards to evaluate your tools?"

He looked startled, then chuckled. "Of course. They must function for the purpose I need and be reliable, from a credible service or source."

"Okay," she said, nodding. "Do you need a tool to know yourself better, and to what end? Is the tool in these books proven to be reliable? Who is the service or source for them?"

Zach's eyes flashed with the challenge. He looked at Declan as if they could brainstorm answers together, but Declan's tone was matter of fact as he said, "I'm being honest here—I have no need of a way to focus on myself or evaluate and categorize other people by a number and personality types. It never occurred to me. Someone already identified me for career strengths in an evaluation in college, and I didn't think the results reflected much about who I am."

"Okay, I admit, I wasn't looking for that tool either," said Zach.

"Have you checked into the reliability of the tool that isn't really a tool?" asked Mercedes.

With a sigh, Zach said, "No, but they used it in training materials for the firm. They've screened it."

Mercedes and Jana exchanged knowing looks. Declan said, "Okay, okay, show us how you are both smarter than Jill."

"The teachings in these books and classes vary," Mercedes said. "Relevant academic circles don't widely accept the material. Some leaders are into psychotherapy and others are about spirituality. In a public interview that you can watch online the person who started the movement admitted to making up the personality teachings via channeling or automatic writing, which is giving yourself over as a medium to allow a spirit guide to take over. One proponent of the personality 'tool' uses abusive techniques in his writing and blogs to gaslight and insult Christians."

Zach studied her face in starlight and Declan quipped, "This gives a whole new meaning to Jill's insistence that the teachings are 'ancient.' The devil and other evil spirits have been around since the creation of the world."

"And it explains why it is not religion-neutral," said Jana. "It's popular with women's groups, and in my experience, they're notorious for opening doors to false teaching. It is wrecking marriages and relationships, as if those weren't in enough trouble already."

When Zach remained silent, Mercedes reached out to touch his hand. "Look, Jana and I only want to share what we've learned and encourage you to investigate, as an attorney would, using primary sources, data points, coherence, and context to prove your case. Put this on trial. If we're wrong, show us."

A group of employees with Lenoir, Bassett, and Madigan gathered around the flames of a firepit behind the beach house. They greeted Zach, Mercedes, Jana, and Declan as they crossed the boardwalk from the darkened beach, waving them over to join them. The four friends walked over to be sociable, and Declan asked what everyone was doing the next day.

Several were going out with the boat the following afternoon, hoping to bring back dinner, and said the group setting out in the morning had already turned in for an early start.

"We should do the same," said Jana, yawning, and she wished the group a good night.

Zach clasped Mercedes' hand to walk her to her room but turned back when one man at the fire pit called to him. "I almost forgot, Zach. Mr. Lenoir asked us to let you know he'd like to meet with you tonight. He'll be in his office until late, catching up on business he left while traveling. Do you know where the office is?"

Hesitating, Zach said, "Is it the one in the other house, where we waited to go to training and dinner the past few days?"

"That's the general office for anyone to use," Declan said. "Jill has been there this week. Mr. Lenoir's office is across the hall."

As they passed through the deck doors into the house, Declan kept his voice low to ask, "What do you think he wants that can't wait until tomorrow?"

"I wish I knew," murmured Zach. The living room area loomed in shadows, lit only by a small night lamp on a table by the front door. They walked to it and said goodnight to Zach as he left to take the sidewalk to the next house.

Jana held her fingers to her temples, and Declan asked her if she had a headache. "Yes—yes, ever since we came through the door." She looked at Mercedes. "Do you feel it?"

Mercedes nodded and put her hand on Jana's shoulder. Declan quipped lamely, "You two are sharing headaches now?"

"I don't have one," Mercedes said. "I think I know what's bothering Jana, we just react differently. My heart rate has gone up and I feel—well, alert and wary, like something is off. Listen Jana, I brought over-the-counter pain caplets with me, but they're in the side pocket of my cooler, with my vitamins. I'll go to the kitchen to get them for you, and something to drink. Declan, if you'll walk her upstairs, I'll be there soon."

The door to Mr. Lenoir's office was only half closed, and Zach tapped lightly on the doorframe before standing in it. Mr. Lenoir invited him into the warmly lit, expensively furnished room, and he attempted to look composed, as if there was nothing odd about being summoned to the office in the middle of the night.

As he shook hands with Mr. Lenoir, he felt a presence behind him in the room. A chill ran gooseflesh up his neck. He was about to glance around when Mr. Lenoir pointed to reveal another man and introduced him as part of his security team. The team would monitor both beach houses over the weekend.

Politely, Zach shook hands with the burly man, who went outside the open office door to give them more privacy. The beach houses had a security system, he knew, for guests were warned as to the hours staff would set it. But it was late now, and he was out, so maybe the extra security would allow guests more freedom from the alarms.

"Sit down and make yourself comfortable, Zach," said Mr. Lenoir congenially. He was behind his desk now, pointing to a leather chair. Zach thanked him and looked around. "You have an interest in antique daggers?" he asked, surveying the tastefully displayed collection.

Lenoir chuckled. "Yes. Silver ones, to be specific. I inherited some of these from my family and I discovered others on the antiquities market. I'll stop one day when I find the right one."

Zach stopped looking at the daggers and turned a quizzical expression on Mr. Lenoir. "The right one?"

Lenoir's air became sardonic, and his eyes were those of a man whose mind takes too many dangerous trains of thought. "Yes, a particular one, from my family's history. We never discovered what became of it and I'm uncertain exactly what it looked like. But I'll know it when I have it in my hands. Most people who come into my office for the first time ask me about the framed motto and emblem instead of the daggers, though the motto encompasses my purpose in collecting the daggers. The Latin means 'What nourishes me destroys me.'"

Zach studied the emblem, a torch burning downward, dripping wax, but consuming itself as the flow of wax quenched the flames. He wanted to shudder but held himself in check. This conversation was surreal. It was after midnight, and he was in an office full of silver daggers, ominous mottos, and a man who made him uneasy.

He cleared his throat. "I'm sure you're busy and I don't want to take up your time. One of the other attorneys said you wanted to see me."

"Oh, yes, yes, I do. It will be a challenge to make time to meet in private tomorrow, with all the fishing boat outings and other activities. What are your feelings for Mercedes Ellison?"

Zach blinked, and he grew wary. "I'm a lawyer, not a poet."

Mr. Lenoir belted out a hearty laugh and clapped lightly. "Bravo, Mr. Boone. She is all that, isn't she? I should have been less direct. What I'm asking is, what are your intentions for the future with Miss Ellison if you sign on with Lenoir Bassett and Madigan?"

"I planned to propose to her. But now, she wants to break away for a while, waiting until I'm settled into my career. I realized tonight that she's right. She deserves better than me."

Behind his desk, Lenoir scowled. "Would a partnership make you worthy?"

Zach stared, uncomprehending.

"I see I'm unloading too much on you. Chalk it up to a long day. You are family to me, Mr. Boone. Distant, but related," he said, sliding papers across his desk toward Zach's chair. "I knew you wouldn't believe me, so I had a report done."

Dazed, Zach reached for the papers and scanned them over. It was a DNA analysis. His voice was icy when he asked, "When did you do this?"

"Someone with the firm collected your DNA about a year ago, when you attended the reception to announce the contest you entered. Brilliant conclusion for the case, by the way. My ancestor had the same idea. I have drawn up papers that guarantee that at a certain date in the future, the firm will become Lenoir Bassett Madigan and Boone."

Zach stared at the DNA report, noting where his illegitimate link to the Lenoir family occurred. He kept his fury in check as he slowly said, "This has something to do with Mercedes?"

Lenoir opened his hand in an appeal and sat back in his chair. "She's the icing on your cake," he said wily. "You get what you want—an unheard-of career opportunity and the stunning young lady who has made it all possible. We can go over the details another day."

The leaves of the paper report whispered on their way to the hardwood floor as Zach slowly and deliberately stood up. "After all I endured to get to and get through law school, it turns out that my first job offer isn't about my accomplishments. I'm a victim in a scheme I don't understand, and there are skeletons in my family closet. From my perspective, Mercedes Ellison is the worst thing that ever happened to me. She has ruined my life, yet she's done nothing. I'll be leaving in the morning, Mr. Lenoir, and I never want to hear from you or this firm again."

Before he turned to leave, he caught something ancient, malevolent, and chilling in Mr. Lenoir's eyes. It was not human.

He wondered if one of those old silver daggers would end up in his back as he went to the door.

The security guard was nowhere to be seen in the murky shadows of the hallway. At what point did he leave his post? Unnerved now and shaking from fury and adrenaline, he rushed to go out the front doors and to the relative safety of his friends.

The beach house kitchen had a dim light in the range hood over the grate of the gas cooktop, revealing the comfortable bulky shapes of cabinets and appliances. Tiny lights glowed on the dishwasher as it scrubbed the remnants of dinner from the plates, glasses, and flatware.

Mercedes went to find her soft-sided cooler where she had seen it that afternoon, then sighed. The kitchen staff moved it during the controlled chaos of food preparation and serving for the cookout. But her name tag was on it, so the staff would have left it where she could find it. She pushed aside other bags and boxes on the countertops in case it was behind them.

With a sigh, she set her hands on her hips and stood back to look around. Nothing. Perplexed, she went to investigate the refrigerator, where it would be logical for someone to put a cooler if they assumed it still held food.

"Bingo," she whispered out loud. They stuffed the cooler in the back behind a cake dish, but she recognized the pattern of bright sunflowers against a navy background. It was an effort to pull out the cake container from between the racks and set it on the kitchen island. Then she turned back to the fridge to tug the cooler from the back shelf, set it on the counter, pulled the medicine bottle out, and replace the cake.

From behind, something soft and heavy covered her face and mouth before she could react. She struggled against brutal hands as a gruff voice told someone to be quick with the tranquilizer. A sharp stick of a needle made her try to cry out, but it was a futile moan against the meaty hand that crushed her lips to her teeth. Strong arms were dragging her, and as consciousness drained away, her heart cried out to Jesus to be rescued.

Chapter 9

"She was supposed to be right behind us," Jana whispered as she and Declan came downstairs in search of Mercedes.

"We're in the house, Jana—it's not like she's in any danger here. I'll give you credit. You have a vivid imagination that might come in handy sometimes. Maybe Zach returned and they're talking somewhere. They have a lot to straighten out. Between me and you, I don't think they're going to make it, which is a shame because I really like her."

"Mercedes wouldn't do that," Jana protested. "I mean, yes, she will break up with Zach. She's level-headed and sees the writing on the wall. Besides, she likes him but doesn't love him, I could see that in our conversation about him at lunch today.

Jana rubbed her temples, then said, "But about the medicine for my headache, her priority would be to get that to me, then go off with Zach."

They moved cautiously through the dimly lit house into the kitchen. A soft sided fabric cooler sat askance on the middle island by the refrigerator, and the small plastic bottle of pain relief caplets had rolled off onto the tiled floor.

Jana's hand went to her mouth in dismay. Declan froze, searching for a reasonable explanation for the uncanny scene, but nothing good came to mind.

"Something happened," whispered Jana. "She didn't put the pain reliever and cooler away, and she never even got the water bottles to bring up. Snap a photo of this with your phone."

"What? Why?"

"I don't know. It could be important. She was taking pictures of the white car in case she needed them, too."

Declan took a photo from different angles while Jana looked out the windows into the darkness. She grabbed his arm. "Come on. If she went out the door, she could be in trouble. Remember the guy who was following her?"

"Oh, man, Jana. We'll feel silly when we find out this is nothing sketchy, and I'm blaming the craziness on you. I'm a lawyer, not a loon."

They checked to be sure the security alarm was not set at the kitchen door, then went out into the night. Jana gasped, "Look! This is hers!"

She pointed at the path to the driveway, where a slender cross-body cellphone purse was outlined by moonlight. The strap was ripped from the hook latch on one side. They photographed it with the flash on Declan's camera.

"I can hardly stand to leave it there like that, but if something happened to her and there are prints on the case, we shouldn't disturb evidence," said Jana. She looked toward the parking lot. "We should see if the white car is over there!"

"Okay, okay, I guess you're not crazy after all, but this has permanently upped your level of spookiness," Declan declared as they ran to the public beach access parking. "How often do you watch suspense thrillers and know the end before the characters do?"

They saw the sedan and Jana forgot to answer him. It was the only vehicle in the lot, and they ran to it.

"We've got him! He made the transaction using the beach house facilities, as you predicted, and we can prove he was here. We're going in. Give us about fifteen minutes. Are you at the public access?"

The handsome antiquities specialist stood along the dark tree line against a low tabby wall bordering the vacation house he was watching. He peered through the shadows at the vast building, which seemed to sleep. "I just came up a few minutes ago from the beach, watching the boardwalk for any activity. I heard voices a minute ago and I'm watching now—"

He spun around at the sounds of pounding and saw a couple peering into his rental car. "Mercedes! Are you in there?" cried a young lady.

"Wait, hold on a minute—something happened," he told the man on the other line. "Hold on and listen, I'm leaving the phone on and going to the car. Mercedes' friends are there looking for her." He left the phone on in his raised hands and rushed to the car. "Is something wrong? Can I help?"

"Have you seen Mercedes Ellison? We know you were watching her! She's missing, under suspicious circumstances, and we found her phone with a broken strap on the path. No one can track her," blurted the young man.

"No, I was watching the boardwalk until a few minutes ago. I'm on the white hat side trying to protect her. Tell me why you believe she's missing."

The young woman's voice caught on a sob. Then she said, "She went to the kitchen to get something for my headache, and we thought she would be right behind us. But she didn't come up at a reasonable time, so we went to the kitchen to find her. The cooler wasn't sitting right, and the bottle of pain reliever was on the floor. Outside the door, her cellphone purse broke on the path to the driveway. We touched nothing so evidence is undisturbed. My boyfriend took photos."

The young man with her was already pulling up photos to show. A boat engine came to life at a nearby dock, and they all looked in that direction before locking eyes. "Why would any neighbors take a boat out at this time of night?" asked the young man.

The investigator spoke curtly into his cellphone. "Did you catch that? I'm looking at their photos, and they are on to something. Tell your men not to disturb evidence in the kitchen or the path by the kitchen door until someone evaluates it."

"My team will be there in five minutes, tops. The staff had to leave by eleven tonight, so I have no eyes in the house."

"I keep hearing a boat engine. This couple wants to help, and they shouldn't be in the house right now, so I'm taking them with me to the beach to check it out. I may need a first responder for a medical situation." He ended the call and opened the trunk of the white car, where he unloaded gear, handing the couple flashlights, flares, and towels.

This investigation was at an end tonight.

Zach fought back his rising alarm. Declan was not in their shared room, and Jana and Mercedes' room was empty. He was sure they were tired and on their way to bed when he left for the meeting with Lenoir. He texted Mercedes but got no answer. He tried to call, but there was no response.

He descended the stairs of the silent house, wondering if his friends could have gone back outside by the firepit to wait for him, wanting to hear about the meeting. Maybe Jana had the creeps again and couldn't sleep. He was on the deck to go out and look for them when he was taken into custody of law enforcement while other officers stealthily swarmed into the house.

Wild instinct brought Mercedes to the surface of the sea and helped her fight the black weight of it. Sputtering and coughing, she opened her stinging eyes. She panicked, in total confusion, unable to comprehend the reality of her cold surroundings. Climbing slopes of dark glass carried her up as their foaming crests sprayed against a black sky. She was like a part of a windy race with the stars, and foam blew into her eyes and mouth as her arms flailed.

Her mind screamed that panic would kill her, so she tried to fight it and gulp the next breath of air, listening for any sign of rescue. The hissing waves that tossed her ran under a night wind, muffling all other sounds, but she thought she heard an engine. The only explanation for being here was that she was dumped off a boat, but when she struggled to look around, there was no light to reveal one.

A misty glow in the distance must be the coastline, however, and she felt a surge of hope. She was treading water, desperately floundering as memories more chilling than the deep water returned.

That she was left for dead, to wash up on shore in some tragic story, only strengthened her resolve. There was no chance she could swim the distance to the beach. None. But her fate was never in the hands of her enemies, so she prayed desperately while slapping crests of water threatened to submerge her.

Mercedes gulped and gasped, coming up for a breath of precious salty air, then noticed the cusp of a dorsal fin that glittered briefly in starlight. In an instant, it disappeared in leaping black waves. But the surface of the water beside her bulged and swelled with more power than the waves, breaking with the curved thrust of a slick silver back.

Without thinking, she reached for the moon shaped horn, and it carried her forward. Another slick, rubbery body turned beside her in a rolling dive, and she let go of the dorsal fin when she was half-lifted, half-thrown across the current. Before the ocean threatened to whirl her backwards, Mercedes heard squeals, trills, and whistles. She gasped as the dolphin bumped her and butted her forward from the other side into the white surge.

Instinct made her want to struggle for survival on her own. But she sensed that if she kept her head and let the dolphin pair work together, reaching shallower water and less current was possible. She swam when needed and rolled with them to their own rhythm, elated and barely believing the experience.

Glittering points of light appeared on what must be the beach. Mercedes knew the dolphin pair had pushed her a remarkable distance in a short time, but she fought exhaustion and was uncertain how the drug her attackers injected was affecting her. The dolphins would soon reach their limit on proximity to the shore. With another shove of a powerful silvery body, she glimpsed a dark shape in the water, outlined in the glimmer of starlight, but she went under again, ready for the next toss of her body by the dolphin pair.

This time, the rolling dive sent her bumping into something. Startled, she came to the surface, gasping and flailing. A voice shouted, "It's okay now, Mercedes. Work with me. Can you still swim?"

Dazed, she treaded water and tried to remain calm. Her teeth chattered, and she trembled uncontrollably as her rescuer strapped something buoyant on her. Mercedes knew the soothing voice that assured her she was safe and told her they were only a few feet away from being able to stand on the ocean floor. He asked again if she could swim. She nodded.

Behind them, a series of chirps, clicks, and whistles made her turn. A bottlenose shape seemed to peer at her before it submerged. Two crescent moon fins glittered, and then two tail flukes smacked the water triumphantly.

Mercedes choked on a sob. Her rescuer pulled her around from her grateful goodbye and she swam with the help of the life-saving tube. He stayed beside her and was soon touching the moving ocean floor, walking, pulling her along. Like a jointless rag doll, she floated in sheer exhaustion.

Jana and Declan were up to their hips in water, heedless of the fate of their dinner clothes, waiting to help Mercedes out of the ocean—or pull her body in. Her rescuer stopped within their reach and went to his knees, gasping. Jana sobbed, grabbing to see if Mercedes had a pulse, and Declan cried out with relief when Mercedes started coughing.

Together, they tried to lift her, but her dead weight limply gave way to the black shallows, and she retched sea water. Her rescuer had recovered with enough strength to pitch in, and the three half-carried, half-dragged Mercedes to the spot where their flashlights waited in the sand.

She was shaking uncontrollably when they covered her with an enormous beach towel and her rescuer called someone on his cellphone. His voice was tense while he promised to wait for help to be sent to them. "Get men out to that boat dock *now*!" he shouted. "If the attackers have left, there still may be evidence of the boat being taken out on the water and the victim being on board."

When he hung up, he drew a shaky breath, then said, "An EMT is on his way. It won't be five minutes. Law enforcement is at the beach houses behind us, so look for him crossing the boardwalk."

He plopped down in the sand beside Mercedes. On the other side, Jana was quietly crying and running her fingers through her friend's hair, which hung like tangled golden seaweed. Beside her, Declan was using Jana's phone to text her parents, asking for prayers.

Mercedes trembled, coughed, and sometimes shuddered, but when her rescuer slid close and rubbed the towel over her arm, she smiled weakly. "You're the best part of this nightmare," she said through chattering teeth.

The stars provided just enough light to reveal his impish grin. He leaned closer. "Only if I can be the knight in shining armor who gets the princess. Otherwise, I don't do nightmares. I want to be the man of your best dreams."

Chapter 10

He who fears to suffer suffers from fear.
-French Proverb

At the rental cottage in Bluffton, Josette and Dawson Ellison sat in the small but comfortable living room and handled email and texts. They stepped outside to the courtyard for phone calls. The door to their daughter's bedroom remained closed as she slept well into the day.

In front of them, at the French patio doors, Lois waved and led Jana and Declan into view. They pantomimed whether it was okay to come inside, and Josette rose to let them in.

Lois kept her voice low and said, "I'll let you all introduce yourselves. Aaron and I are grilling dinner in the courtyard tonight, so don't trouble about food."

"Oh, you've been such a blessing! Thank you ever so much." Josette's eyes brimmed with unexpected tears, and she swiped at them quickly. "Dawson and I want to focus on helping Mercedes sort out how to move forward."

"I've made up the extra bedroom in my house. Come stay tonight, if she seems to be okay alone, and if you wish to be close by until she recovers. You have my number, just text if you need anything."

After they exchanged a hug and Josette closed the door, she turned to her husband and guests, who were getting to know one another. They caught her up in low voices, trying not to awaken Mercedes. Jana briefly explained how she and Declan knew their daughter.

"We've reported to the authorities all we know about what happened last night," Declan said solemnly. "It isn't much. But there was an investigation already underway into an unrelated series of crimes, including murder, and things went down with miraculous timing. I admit, I'm still trying to wrap my head around all this."

"I knew something was wrong in that house, and Mercedes felt like something bad was about to happen, minutes before they kidnapped her," said Jana breathlessly, wringing her hands. "You may think I'm a kook, but Mercedes understands."

Josette and Dawson looked at one another and smiled. "We understand, too, Jana," Dawson said slowly. "Sometimes our gifts feel more like a curse. If you live your life seeking Jesus and stay grounded in the reality of His word, you're ready for battle in your spiritual armor."

"Yes, that's it!" whispered Jana. "What happened was so horrible I can't bear to remember it yet, but I'll never regret meeting your daughter. In only a few days, she feels like a sister to me. I love her and I want you to know I plan to stay in touch after we leave. We must get back to Virginia today, but we're going to look for jobs closer to the Lowcountry now."

Declan said, "It's back to the drawing board for me with sending out resumes. But I learned the truth about the company."

"What happened to Zach? Is he okay?" asked Josette.

Declan and Jana looked at one another sadly, and he sighed. "I stayed with him until they let him go last night—uh, early this morning. He told me what he told the authorities, about how he learned he was being used by Lenoir and walked out on him. When Mercedes, Jana, and I weren't anywhere to be found, he came looking, and texted and called Mercedes. But you know how we found her phone, so she couldn't answer. All our stories lined up. He rented a car and left as soon as he could get his bags in it."

Jana clasped her hands, gripping until her knuckles were white, and said, "Zach told us what he told Lenoir—that meeting Mercedes is the worst thing that ever happened to him, and she has ruined his life. He says he never wants to see her again, but I think he's just upset, and he feels guilty, and his family is in upheaval after learning about the illegitimate birth connection to Lenoir's family. He's throwing his fear, grief, and frustration onto Mercedes."

They all turned when they heard a gasp. A disheveled Mercedes stood at her open bedroom door, close to the living room. She wore a wrinkled tee shirt and jean shorts.

Jana jumped up and ran to her. "Mercedes! Did you hear us?"

Mercedes nodded. Jana hugged her, then quickly pulled away, remembering how bruised and sore her friend was from her kidnapping and from being bumped by the dolphins. They walked into the living room, where Jana made a place to sit with her. Josette went to the kitchen to get hot herbal tea for her daughter and asked what she could bring for everyone else.

"Did you say Zach is a relative of Lenoir's?" rasped Mercedes.

Declan and Jana nodded, knowing she would comprehend how important the revelation was. A marriage between Mercedes and Zach would tie an ancient enemy to his prey.

"He told me about his meeting with Lenoir last night," said Declan. "The office creeped him out. Lenoir collects antique silver daggers as if he's obsessed with them, and said he'll know the right one when he gets it. And he talked about an engraving display in his office, with a Latin motto and a burning torch turned upside down. It means—"

"*What nourishes me destroys me,*" said Josette, Dawson, and Mercedes in unison. Wide-eyed, Josette froze on her way to her daughter with hot tea. Dawson ran his hands over his face. "Unbelievable. He's spent years and untold amounts of money, looking for the dagger."

Josette took the tea to Mercedes and sat down with a stunned look. Seeing the confusion on their guests' faces, Dawson said, "My wife and I have knowledge of the silver dagger Lenoir wants. He will never get his hands on it, even if he gets out of prison. As for the engraving, it's a popular Elizabethan motto taken from a Shakespearean play. There's an old tomb on Hilton Head Island decorated with the torch burning downward, consuming itself. It can represent unrequited passion and love, but the concept also applies to mystical, metaphysical, and political things. I believe I know what it means to Lenoir, but I won't speak for him. I wish we knew who left the antique cedar chest at an estate auction for our daughter to find and reclaim for our family. These things tie together, I just don't know how."

Declan and Jana sat quietly, taking in the new perspective. Reaching for Jana's hand, Declan said, "What Mr. Ellison said about that motto reminded me of the topic you and Mercedes tried to warn me and Zach about, with the personality books. Carrying a torch for ourselves is a fire that will consume us."

He cleared his throat and ventured, "Mr. Ellison, Zach said something else happened that changed his mind about the supernatural realm. I wonder what you think about it. When Zach refused to take part in a plot against Mercedes, he saw a look pass in Mr. Lenoir's eyes that he claims was not human. I suggested it was madness, but Zach says no, it was an evil entity within Mr. Lenoir. You must understand, Mr. Ellison, Zach is one of the most level-headed, logical thinkers I know. Yet, he remains convinced and shaken."

With a meaningful look at his wife and daughter, Dawson blew out a breath. "It sounds like Zach glimpsed an invisible world he probably suspected the existence of, but he needed proof. It will open him up to accepting and understanding what comes next in his life. He's being prayed for, and the Lord's ways are not our ways. Zach's world is upended, and he needs a friend to talk to who was there with him. I know you'll be that friend. Jana can help him, too."

"Mr. Ellison, do you believe what Zach saw is real?" ventured Jana.

"I know it was," answered Dawson. "I've seen it myself."

Mercedes brushed her tousled hair, taming it into a ponytail to walk with Declan and Jana to their car. She wasn't sure how to say goodbye to friends whose persistence had likely saved her life, and they were all still emotionally shaky. She fussed over how they should stay another night in town to rest, but Declan claimed to be like a cat on a hot tin roof, his mind churning with all the implications of what happened. He felt the drive would do him good while Jana napped, then they would eat somewhere and switch so Declan could sleep.

After promising to text her when they stopped and when they arrived at Jana's house, they pulled away. Mercedes stood watching, letting the warmth of the sunshine soothe her sore muscles.

Hearing a yap behind her, she turned to look down the sidewalk. Quincy waved, and she burst out laughing, which made her grasp her bruised ribs.

He chuckled as he came to stand in front of her. His hand looped through a lavender leash that shimmered with glitter in the sun. At the end of the leash was a dog that looked like an imaginative stuffed animal wearing a bejeweled collar and bows in its ears.

From Quincy's carpenter shorts pocket, a pink polka-dot doggie waste bag hung, ready to fill. The sight made Mercedes laugh again. "Ouch," she gasped, putting her hand to her waist.

"I would rush to your aid, but I'm already claimed by Bijou here," he said, with a regal wave to the tiny dog. "In case your French is rusty, Bijou means 'jewel.'"

Hearing her name, Bijou jerked her head up, turning an adoring gaze to Quincy. Mercedes continued to fight off laughter.

"It's so nice to meet you, Bijou," she said, though her voice was still raspy. The tiny brown eyes looked up into hers and melted her heart. "Oh..." she breathed.

Quincy picked up the dog and held it in his arms. "Bijou lives just down the road, beside the home where I rented a backyard carriage house apartment," he said. "Her owner is a senior citizen who sprained an ankle, so I offered to walk with her."

"She is a blessed little girl in so many ways," said Mercedes. "There seems to be no end to your list of good deeds."

He grinned but then turned serious. "How are you today?"

"A little better, with mom and dad here, and Declan and Jana stopped by. I heard some hard things from them, but it's part of getting to the other side."

Quincy's eyes studied her. They were intensely blue and always made her stomach flutter pleasantly.

She glanced down at Bijou in his arms and reached to caress her ears. "Can you join us for dinner tonight? Mom and Dad will call you to ask, so I'll let them know I talked to you. Lois, my landlady, and Aaron, the contractor here who is also her friend, are grilling out back in the courtyard."

"Are you inviting me, or Bijou?"

She looked up at him and smiled. "You, of course. Lois' place is a no pet's zone."

"I'd love to come. Text me when you know a time. Otherwise, I'll show up early and be a nuisance."

"Show up early and be a nuisance."

Mercedes, Quincy, and her parents opened the cottage doors to the courtyard and strolled over to where Lois and Aaron waited for seafood and steaks to come off the grill. Lois came forward to introduce herself and Aaron to the newcomer, Quincy. "So glad you could join us!" she said, shaking his hand. "You must be the one who's renting the carriage house a few doors down at the Calloway's place."

"Yes, and my name is Quincy Holmwood. Thanks so much for the hospitality. I'll be around for at least the summer, so we're neighbors."

"It's a pleasure to have you and we're glad you joined us. Looks like Aaron is about to serve food from the grill. He'll say grace and we'll choose what we want to eat."

Aaron's deep voice resonated with thanks and gratitude, and there was a bustle of activity as everyone picked up their plates to fill them.

"It sounds like Quincy is not a stranger to the Ellison family," ventured Lois.

"That's right," Dawson replied. "Our families go back several generations. We've been to a lot of places in the world together. Quincy's family has an interest in archaeology, and they've been part of some important discoveries."

"Oh, my, I've never met an archaeologist before!" exclaimed Lois. "What are you digging up here in Bluffton?"

Everyone laughed, and Quincy said, "I'm an independent contractor, working with museums, private collectors, and dig site consulting. I just finished a contract in the field of Antiquities as an investigator, but that was a special case. The world has changed dramatically, so I've reevaluated my goals and settled here in America to live near the Ellisons. I work mostly from home, but it's a busy career. I'm a citizen, born here, and my mother is American. But she married my dad, who is British, and I spent most of my life there or traveling to work wherever the archaeology led us."

"What qualifies as an antiquity? I'm pretty old, myself," joked Aaron.

"Some countries say only fifty years old, others recently set it at one hundred. But I prefer to work with ancient artifacts, from places I've been. I took on the job that affected Mercedes only because I knew the importance of the crimes committed. I've been on the trail of Stanley Lenoir and his partners for a while."

Lois raised her brows and nodded slowly. "I see. You were working on the island last night. Do you drive a white car?"

Mercedes burst out laughing and touched Quincy's arm. "I was unnerved by being followed and asked Lois if anyone living on the street drives a white sedan. They were watching out for me."

Quincy laughed and then sobered. "The officers I was working for had me in a rental car for anonymity, not understanding Mercedes as I did. But God works in mysterious ways. Mercedes showed the car to her friends, and they came running to it to look for her when she was missing. The car was a point for us to meet and find her. But I'll be driving my own vehicle from now on."

After dinner, Lois and Aaron sent Quincy and the Ellisons off to relax. Dawson went to talk with Mercedes' brother on the phone, but Josette insisted on helping Lois and Aaron clean up. Mercedes answered a text from Jana saying she and Declan had eaten and exhaustion had caught up with Declan, so she would drive the rest of the way home while he snored.

Quincy said, "Seems like a shame to waste this perfectly magnificent swimming pool. My swimsuit is in my gym bag in your cottage. How about it?"

Startled, Mercedes put her hand on her heart. In her mind, black waves encompassed her, and currents pulled her under. The hiss of surf running in the wind filled her ears.

"Mercedes? What is it?"

She passed her hand over her eyes and gave him a weak smile. "It may be too soon for me to swim."

He studied her, nodded, then said, "Maybe. But maybe you need to try." He took her arm and led her to the side of the pool. "It's safe, Mercedes. Look, the lights will soon be on, and it will glow turquoise. No dark waves. And best of all, I'll be with you. I won't let go."

With a reluctant nod, she followed him inside the cottage to change. By the time they were out again, the courtyard and the pool lay in tranquil twilight. Quincy took her hand and led her to the curved stairs and down into the shallows.

There was no sound of crashing waves, and no wind blew salty sea foam in her ears. The water glowed, clear and inviting. She tried to relax, though it hurt at first to stretch some of her muscles. "I'm still sore, so I'll just float."

"So, you aren't used to having a six to twelve foot long, up to four-hundred-pound animal shoving you around?"

"Don't make me laugh, it hurts!"

"Come here, this is therapy. Stretch the muscles slowly and float. I'll pull you around and you tell me when it's too much."

Mercedes gave in, looking up to the first faint stars and the silver cusp of the moon. The only sounds were the homey, distant voices of her parents laughing with Lois and Aaron, some people on the street, and the trickle of water from the pool filter.

Almost whispering, Quincy said, "Good thing your parents didn't tell Lois the entire story about our family histories, and she didn't pick up on my name. She might be nervous to know I'm named for Quincey Morris and there was once speculation that our families were among those who inspired heroic characters in classic horror novels."

Mercedes closed her eyes and smiled, floating easily as he kept his arms under her back. "You don't know Lois. She would be undaunted."

He chuckled. "In that case, we're all set for an exciting summer. What do you say, can we hang out together again, like old times?"

The dreams she had of him the past few nights washed over her like the silky water, and she thought of the messages in the old cedar chest, with the convicting words of her Great-Great Grand Aunt's journal. She murmured, "I'm not running anymore, trying to steer by my own stars. I'll face life with the help the Lord provides. I'm Mercedes Ellison, and I can't escape my destiny."

To the Reader

Did you like this novel? You can continue the adventures of Mercedes Ellison in the Strange Sands Suspense Series. Remember to help other readers by sharing your review!

There is a list of **Resources** for readers who enjoyed this novella series and want to investigate certain aspects of it. For Book Clubs, there is a page called **Discussion Topics** to help leaders guide conversations and glean more spiritual insight from the stories. And if you're a romantic, learn more about Alljoy Beach[1] in Bluffton, SC.

Stay updated with me via my fun-packed author newsletter and websites at Southern Sky Publishing[2] and Pamela Poole Fine Art[3], or join me on YouTube[4], Goodreads[5] and BookBub[6].

---

1. https://www.locallifesc.com/wayback-lowcountry-alljoy-beach/

2.   http://www.southernskypublishing.com

3.   http://www.pamelapoole.com

4.   https://www.youtube.com/channel/UC9aV3zHRlASXUUBEF7xbT9Q

5.   https://www.goodreads.com/author/show/3934732.Pamela_Poole

6.   https://www.bookbub.com/profile/pamela-poole

Discussion Topics

If you read the first novella in this series, The Old Cedar Chest, what was your impression of the Prologue event?

Readers know that there are more dysfunctional relationships around us than positive, healthy ones. Whatever situation we find ourselves in, what can we do to turn things around for ourselves and for others who need to see a good influence? Can we do this on our own, or do we need Jesus to make a way when we can't see the next step?

Like Mercedes in this novella series, have you ever tried to steer your own course in life to avoid living a life surrendered to the destiny Jesus planned for you? How did He bring you back?

How many Bible references in this story did you look up?

Resources

Biblical and Historical Perspectives on the Supernatural

There are so many! Here are the ones where I find the most helpful research material for both reliable, quick references and for in-depth Bible Study and Biblical Worldview writing. I'm sure readers have favorites they would add to this list, but there may be a new one for you on this list.

YouTube has many podcast interviews and conference presentations with Dr. Michael S. Heiser about the Bible, but those who want to dig deeper will discover a lot of extra material and primary sources on this scholar's main website. I highly recommend his book *Supernatural*, which I have, and his videos on the Divine Council and Cosmic Geography:
Dr. Michael S. Heiser[7]

Answers for challenging science and worldview questions:
Answers In Genesis[8]
Cross Examined (Frank Turek)

---

7. https://drmsh.com/

8. https://answersingenesis.org/

Christian Women's Podcast for Apologetics and Worldview

Alicia Childers (former Christian singer with ZOEgirl)
Melissa Dougherty (Christian Apologetics podcast and
author of <u>Happy Lies</u>)

About the Author

Pamela Poole writes inspirational mystery and suspense that explore the intersection of faith, history, and the unseen spiritual realm. Her stories are grounded in a clear Christian worldview and shaped by a deep respect for both historical preservation and biblical truth.

Pamela writes inspirational stories that bring together Christian faith, historic places, and hidden truths. Her novels reveal how the past can press into the present, where faith becomes essential to discernment and courage. Her characters are ordinary people facing extraordinary challenges, learning to trust Jesus when darkness threatens and answers are not easily found.

Pamela is the author of the Strange Sands Suspense series and the Painter Place Saga, blending richly detailed settings with themes of calling, obedience, redemption, and spiritual warfare. Her fiction offers clean, thought-provoking suspense designed both to engage the imagination and to encourage the heart.

When she isn't writing, Pamela enjoys research, painting in her art studio and on location along the Southern coast and making memories with her family and friends.

Readers and art enthusiasts alike can enjoy her YouTube channel[9] for painting demos and art education presentations.

To enjoy the latest content, sign up for her fun-filled newsletters and follow Pamela Poole Fine Art[10] and Southern Sky Publishing[11].

---

9. https://www.youtube.com/channel/UC9aV3zHRlASXUUBEF7xbT9Q

10. https://www.pamelapoole.com/

11. https://www.southernskypublishing.com/

The Strange Sands Novella Series

The Old Cedar Chest, Strange Sands Suspense 1
Hilton Head

An antique cedar hope chest.
A hidden panel.
A century-spanning vendetta.

Mercedes Annalee Ellison held her Great-Great-Grand Aunt's fragile journal and a tattered manila envelope, puzzling about whether these items would change her life. Her intuition screamed that they would, and the way they had come into her possession would make any skeptic pause. She wanted to bolt, to flee what loomed ahead.

Distractions were not welcome in her life right now. She was an architectural historian with three great jobs lined up for the summer—and a problem with her boyfriend.

When she finds herself entangled in a diabolical vendetta against her family over disputed land in England, Mercedes franticly searches for answers about why she is a target for something that happened back in the year 1900. A man murdered her ancestor, Claire Ellison, one night in an eerie storm, and only a miracle will save Mercedes from the same fate. Can she survive and accept her destiny as part of the legendary Ellison family?

The Hidden Hallway, Strange Sands Suspense 2
Savannah

An antebellum house.
A hidden hallway.
A tale of passion and revenge.

As an architectural historian, Mercedes Ellison is hired by Tammy and Clayton Popplewell to guide them as they register and renovate an antebellum house in the beautiful Southern city of Savannah, Georgia. But she knows this is not the boring job she hoped for when she arrives to find the local police there on the first day. As Mercedes investigates the history of the property and neighbors seek her out with a strange Civil War Era tale of passion and revenge, she works to uncover a terrifying darkness and help the Popplewell couple make the house into the inn where they hope to share light - before the Popplewells give up and she loses the job.

The Freedom Staircase, Strange Sands Suspense 3
Charleston

An Enduring Lowcountry Plantation.
A Legendary Patriot Refuge.
A Last Stand for Freedom.

It thrilled Mercedes Ellison to be chosen to work as an architectural historian for Majestic Oaks, a plantation that endured and survived wars on American soil. The stately Georgian mansion features the Freedom Staircase, where legendary patriots stopped for refuge in their roles with the Continental Army in the American Revolution. Her client needs help to keep the plantation he inherited, which is steeped in the history of the Lowcountry of South Carolina, home of the Swamp Fox and four signers of the Declaration of Independence.

There are also some unsolved mysteries on the property. Bringing them to light will help her client, and she finds clues in a secret passage used by the patriots. But then her archenemy dies in jail and his son hunts her down. Can she make a last stand for freedom from the vengeful vendetta that began with the murder of her ancestor on a stormy night in England?

The Dark Passage, Strange Sands Suspense 4
Bluffton

A bizarre souvenir from far away.
A painting of a pagan ritual.
An evil presence unlimited by time and space.

An aging adventurer named Doran Marlowe once led missionary teams to unreached people groups. His unusual travel souvenirs are kept in a shuttered passage from his rambling house to his art studio, where his paintings begin to take on an unearthly character.
When Mercedes hears Doran's sister screaming on the veranda and runs to help her, she's plunged into another bizarre mystery. Did a menacing presence follow her from an archaeology site she worked at in the past?

The Devil's Drawer, Strange Sands Suspense 5
Beaufort

An ominous oath taken for personal privilege.
An enigmatic artifact unbound by time and place.
An evil consequence for generations.

A chilling mystery unfolds at Seashell Cottage as architectural historian Mercedes Ellison stumbles upon an ominous black cabinet decorated with ancient Egyptian symbols. Delivered under the cover of darkness, this enigmatic artifact pulls her and her client into a web of secrets that stretches across generations.

As they delve deeper, a private investigator friend joins them in unraveling the sinister connection between the cabinet and a long-buried family oath to a clandestine society. With blood as the ultimate spiritual currency, they must confront the haunting legacy of a deceased ancestor whose evil choices ripple through time, binding Mercedes' client in ways they never imagined.

This gripping story is filled with suspense, intrigue, and revelations. As a Christian, Mercedes knows that Jesus reverses curses. But will her client come to know this before it is too late?

Grab your copy today and join Mercedes on this thrilling adventure!

New in 2026!

The Black Hourglass, Strange Sands Suspense 6
St. Augustine

In the shadow lies the truth.
A hidden letter.
A stolen fortune.
A secret that refused to stay buried.

Quincy Holmwood thought his work in St. Augustine was over until a cryptic message from a church archivist pulled him back into a mystery from 1688. Can he resist a search for the truth left by a murdered friar about hidden evidence of a crime against the Crown, committed by a powerful group of colonial settlers of America's oldest city? The trail of clues had endured for the courageous man of a future generation who was bold enough to follow them.

With his fiancée, **Mercedes Ellison**, and a small archaeology team, Quincy races to decode symbols tied to a forgotten brotherhood whose emblem—the **black hourglass**—marks the flow of time the brotherhood believed was under their control.

The brotherhood's final heir is watching his progress. And he never wants the past to come to light.

As accidents turn deadly, Quincy must rely on his faith and the conviction that he is the one the friar believed would someday reveal the truth.

What was hidden in darkness was never meant to stay there.

Other Books by Pamela Poole
Southern Sky Publishing[12]

The Painter Place Saga
Painter Place
Hugo
Jaguar
Landmark

3 Legends of Painter Place (short stories)
The Wind Songs of the Marsh
King's Ransom
The Castaway and the Mermaid

Southern Sky Devotional
Inspired Artistry—Embracing the Creative Calling

---

12. https://www.southernskypublishing.com/

www.ingramcontent.com/pod-product-compliance
Lightning Source LLC
Chambersburg PA
CBHW020655180626
46816CB00003B/1300